Father Bill

Wynn Melton

Father Bill

Wynn Melton

Mockingbird Lane Press

Father Bill
Copyright © 2018 Wynn Melton

This is a work of fiction. While some names, characters, places, and incidents are the product of the author's imagination, some are accurate, but are used to further the story. The publisher does not have any control over and does not assume any responsibility for author or third-party websites or their content.

Mockingbird Lane Press—Maynard, Arkansas

ISBN: 978-1-64316-785-5

Library of Congress Control Number in publication data

0 9 8 7 6 5 4 3 2 1

www.mockingbirdlanepress.com

Cover graphics: Jamie Johnson

Thank you to Ruth Featherstone, Susan Neuman, and Venita Griffin for their encouragement.

Chapter 1

Just ordained, young Reverend William McHeck drove south on US Highway 67 toward his first assignment as pastor at St. Francis of Assisi Parish located in the foothills of the Ozarks. Most men from his class received assistant pastor assignments or administrative duties, but no, he was so proud to receive his papers making him the only one in his class to immediately become a pastor of a church.

With the car windows down and the air blowing through, just below Greenville he turned off Highway 67 to the right on state road FF. He saw no one in front of him or behind so he released his emotions bursting forth with "glory, glory, hallelujah. Glory, glory, hallelujah. Glory, glory, Priest McHeck....Father Bill...is..." He couldn't think of anything to rhyme with either McHeck or Bill so he dropped it, but gave the steering wheel a celebrating slap as he declared. "Did well in my class. The Archbishop took a shine to me. I've really got it. I'll be the best darn pastor in these hills that St. Francis ever had."

The seven miles from Highway 67 rushed by and he saw his next turn onto State Road PP. It was narrower than Highway FF.

It was a Monday with no cars in sight. He recalled back in his school days he was known as Hotrod Bill. He only tapped the brakes to make the left turn and the speed caused the tires to squeal on the black top. Corrected, his arms came up and hands gripped in a winner's salute as his foot stepped down on the gas pedal like a crazy teenager. Celebration time was his. He could see in the distance, over the tree line, a cross yet many miles away. In the desolate area of post oak trees, brush and red clay dotted with cedars he assured himself that it was St. Francis, his parish. He was almost home.

The blacktop curved left and right plus up and down the foothills. He took deep breaths to inhale the fresh, country air that filled his lungs. Again he tried, "Glory, glory, hallelujah. Glory, glory, hallelujah. Glory, glory, hallelujah, Father Bill is moving on."

A car coming in the opposite direction in his lane and only few hills away sped toward him. When they both drove down the next hill and arrived at the top of the next, the car was on the right side of the road. He breathed a sigh of relief. Topping the next hill, it was again headed right for him in his lane.

He slowed, making the sign of the cross just before they met at the top of the next hill.

With the window down the stout, middle-aged, woman driver in the other car slowed and shouted, "Pig. Pig. Pig." He was crushed. Possibly she didn't notice his new, white collar. There was no respect in her voice.

Always fast with responses, he wasn't taking that kind of greeting from anyone, so at the top of his lungs he bellowed, "Ol' hog, ol' hog."

The cars whished past each other. The verbal slam caused him to slow a bit. Two more hills and he hit the brakes hard to come to a screeching halt. A mother hog was standing only inches off the blacktop while her five little pigs rooted around right in the middle of the road.

His hands flew to his head as he said, "Oh, God forgive me." Immediately he wished to someday to find the woman and apologize.

Time meant nothing. He sat there fascinated as he watched the adorable little guys until they followed their mother into the woods. The fear passed and he thanked God for the experience. It was a real treat for a guy born and raised in a city. Relaxed he sang, "Oh, yes, green acres is the place for me. It is where I'm assigned to be. Land spreading out so far and wide, you can keep the cities. Just give me the open countryside."

Stepping on the gas again he knew the cross would only be a few miles ahead. He could see the steeple. A couple more hills and curves and the steeple appeared taller. Soon he was able to detect the entire tall steeple made of bricks.

The desire to beat his chest was there. The steeple could only mean a much larger parish than was anticipated.

On top of the next hill he was able to view more of the impressive steeple. Filled with joy he proclaimed, "Bill, you lucky son-of-a-gun. If only they could see you now."

A sharp turn, almost a one hundred and eighty degree, and the forest again blocked his view. A straight-away stretched in front of him for almost a mile and then climbed up another steep hill.

Near the top, the road was blocked by a small herd of cows. He sat patiently in his car. In front of him in plain view was a very small church building with a totally out of proportion tall brick steeple.

An old farmer sauntered over to say, "Suppose they're still waitin'. These dang cows done broke down the fence and was in the cemetery grazin'. I be back up when I get 'em home. 'Specting you yesterday, they was."

To confirm his belief, Father Bill asked, "So. Is this St. Francis?"

A stream of tobacco spit to the side, he replied, "Yep. Shore is. Gruder's my name. I was baptized here. So was my paw and grand-paw. Been here a long time."

Father Bill extended his hand out the window, "Bill McHeck. The new pastor. I'm curious. Why the small building and such a tall steeple?"

Mr. Gruder stepped back with arms stretched and hands in his pockets to explain, "Well, as I understand it, back when it was built they made a mistake when they ordered dem bricks. After they gots the building as big as they needed, they kept on stacking bricks until they's all used up. Country folks don't waste nothin'."

"Now reckon you'd better git on up there. They's waitin' to bury ol' Mr. Peters so theys can get back to their chores. They gonna be darn glad to see ya."

He drove the cows across the road allowing Father Bill to continue on.

The funeral director rushed to greet him and suggested a proper introduction could wait. "They're all inside and ready."

Father Bill proceeded up the aisle, past the casket, to the altar and began the Funeral Mass.

After the last song was over, he took the lead going outside to stand and wait for the casket.

In the corner of his eye he saw a very large, black and white country dog headed in his direction. Father Bill, having had a bad experience with a dog as a child was truthfully scared of all dogs. This large dog totally frightened him. A decision must be made. He chose to stand very still wishing the dog to pass. He was so still he believed that were he in the city a pigeon might land on his shoulder.

He dared only take short breaths. He watched the casket with the pall-bearers and the dog approach him. His heart was beating fast. He dared not look, but thought the old dog was so close he could smell him.

Country dogs are, in most cases, just happy country dogs.

4

Old Dude first sniffed Father Bill's leg. It didn't quite smell right to him. Most statues didn't have that odor but why take a chance. Old Dude made the decision to mark him as his territory. With heisted leg he relieved himself.

In the casket, ol' Mr. Peters was jostled and turned about like an earthquake as the pallbearers attempted, but could not contain their laughter.

At the luncheon that followed, Father Bill was welcomed by all but never again did he experience anything close to the warm, wet welcome Old Dude gave him that spring morning.

Chapter 2

Quaintberg, just off Highway PP, needed no map. The blacktop stopped just past the churchyard. Across the road from the church was Bleu's General Store and post office housed together. Emmie Lou Bleu was the post mistress. She and husband, Rob, ran the general store. The building was weathered white and two stories. Rob and Emmie Lou lived on the second floor. Weekend hours for the general store were 8 'til noon on Saturday. Sundays it was opened after the 8 am Mass and closed as soon as the last customer checked out. Down Quaintberg Road were three farms and four house trailers sitting on small acreage.

Most residents rose early to go to Sallow, Piedmont or Greenville to work. Some drove as far as Poplar Bluff for employment. Farming was dying in the area but several hung on because it was the only way of life they knew.

There was a mixture of religions, but other than Catholics, they went to Javelle or Sallow to worship.

Masses scheduled on Wednesday and Friday morning was only attended by three or four elderly women and Mr. Gruder. The little church was only a third full at the 8 a.m. Mass on Sunday and consisted of mostly the elderly. Number one on Father Bill's to-do list was to find those who were not attending Mass and bring them home. He believed he must become a fisherman for men...Catholic men.

Fishing could be the answer as he figured all or most country men fished. This was not going to be easy for him since he had never fished, but he did love challenges.

He returned from shopping in Sallow and loaded his new fishing equipment in the car trunk along with three sandwiches and four sodas. Not wishing to make mistakes, it was a must he first fish alone to hone the new skill. He pondered how difficult could it be? Fish brains were small if they had any. They spent all the time in the water searching for food. His equipment was new and the salesclerk assured him with a smile it was the latest on the market. To find water to fish was next on his list.

Quaintberg Road ended after crossing a shallow creek at the gate of Becker's farm. Back at Highway PP he turned right. It was only a quarter of a mile before he spied a long, one lane dirt road dividing a field of corn.

Slowing down, he could see what might be a lake or pond at the far end. He backed up and turned to check it out. It was a small lake with a fair size clearing on one side.

Not only did he find water but a rowboat was tied to a stump for him to use. He reasoned, This is good. I can row out to deep water to catch the big one to impress them with my tale after the next Mass. Maybe even have a picture made to send the Bishop.

Attempting to remain in the sun for warmth, he rowed out toward the south end. Satisfied he was in the right spot, the boat was allowed to slightly float while he struggled to bait the hook. It was a mistake not to have asked the salesclerk when it was appropriate to use each colored worm and how to apply it to the hook. In the paper bag was some two inch black plastic worms with tiny white spots, green plastic worms with yellow stripes about four inches long or the nine inch red plastic worms with blue spots. It could only be decided if he thought like a fish. Black, no. It could be hard to see in the murky water. Green and yellow didn't look appetizing. Taking the red worm with blue spots could be right for the morning snack.

The other concern was how to attach the worm to the hook. Trying to thread the worm on the hook caused many pricks to his fingers. The answer could be with the nine inch worm and a sailor's knot to secure it to the hook.

With the rod held upright he did what he one time saw on TV...flip the line back and then forward. His first cast didn't go forward but caught on a limb of a willow tree hanging out over the water. Releasing the hook, he rowed out a few more feet before casting again. Again it didn't return but caught in his pant leg. Holding it more to the side and away from him was successful. When he began to reel it back in it didn't move easily. He rowed over and pulled harder. With some struggling the catch was in view. On the hook was a small water soaked chunk of wood.

He'd made another mistake. The red and white plastic ball should be used to keep the hook off the bottom. It was attached and he cast again.

Patience was never his strong point but now he must wait for the fish to see the pretty worm and swim over for a late breakfast.

The warm sun relaxed him. Laying the rod and reel in the bottom of the boat he questioned, did all men fish to catch fish or for some was it a just a getaway to relieve the stress of life. With his cares released he began to nod only to be awakened by the sound of an old farm truck.

A man stepped out of his truck, walked toward him and called, "What are you doing out there?"

Father Bill, doing his best to sound country, called back, "Howdy. Beautiful day, ain't it? Great for fishing. Care to join me?"

The old guy laughed, "You're asking me to join you?"

With the rod and reel secure in the boat Father Bill began

to row toward the old man. "You just wait right there. I've got extra soda, a couple sandwiches and extra equipment. If you never fished before I'll help you."

Shaking his head, the old man said, "Well, I'll be danged. Just suppose I might do it," and tossed his jacket in the cab of the truck.

Near shore Father Bill stood and held up his equipment to say, "Tell you what. You can use my equipment since it's already baited. I'll do another."

The red worm swinging in the air caught the old man's eye and caused him to laugh. That was great since not much was happening in his life to cause laughter.

His comments were friendly when he said, "Bet you never caught a fish on that equipment. At least not in water like this. If you wanna really catch some fish you need the right stuff."

He showed Father Bill how to cut fishing poles from willow trees. Next Father Bill learned how to string the line on the new pole and secure the hook, weight and float. A shovel from the bed of the old man's truck was used to dig for worms to put into a rusty bucket.

It occurred to Father Bill that in the excitement that they forgot the introductions. "I'm Father Bill McHeck, the new pastor at St. Francis. I don't think I've seen you at Mass?"

Somehow it tickled the old man and he responded, "Reckon you won't be either. I'm Baptist. Rudolph Meyer is the name. They call me Rudy."

"Best maybe call me Bill."

"Nope. Got respect. Father Bill or Father McHeck. Take your choice."

"I like Father Bill, if it's okay with you."

"So-kay with me, Father Bill. Now let's go fishing."

Most of their catch was small but they released all back

into the water. Each enjoyed the remainder of the day more than either had done for many a month.

It was near three p.m. when Father Bill said, "This has been perfect. I must find the owner and thank him. Do you happen to know where I could find him? I'd like to do it again someday."

Mr. Meyer's grin was wide as he chuckled. "Any time you like, Father Bill. Guess I forgot to tell you. When I saw your car I was wondering who was trespassing on my property so I come looking."

"How about that. Now that I've fished on your property, I would be pleased to take you to dinner."

As they packed the things in the back of the old pickup Mr. Myers explained, "Wife died a couple years back. Tonight I was planning to go into Sallow to Barb's Café to eat. She's got a catfish special today. Don't feel like cooking. Eat out lots."

"Cooking for one isn't easy...so is it going to be to Barb's Café for us? Could you come up to the house say about four thirty and I'll drive?"

Pulling the door shut on his truck Mr. Meyer said, "Only if you let me pay for my own. I don't like being indebted."

Father Bill gave him the thumbs up sign and stood watching him back up and leave. He waited until some dust cleared before he followed.

Now buddies, they fished together, often ate together, helped each other when needed and together took rides over the back country roads. Father Bill gained a wealth of knowledge about the area listening to Mr. Meyer recall past-gone days. On their day trips Mr. Myer began to sing and teach Father Bill to sing the old, old church songs from when he was a kid.

After a few weeks Mr. Myers stopped riding over to visit.

Father Bill drove to his house several times but no one was at home.

Two weeks went by before Father Bill's doorbell rang. Opening the door a middle aged couple he didn't recognize stood on his porch. "Come on in," he said.

They were nervous and gave thought about entering a priest's home. Finally the man said, "Go ahead, Wilma. He invited us in."

It was in silence as they took seats on the couch. Father Bill sat in a chair in front of them. The woman, taking a handkerchief from her purse, began to cry. The man put his arm across her shoulders and pulled her to him before he announced, "Wilma's father died yesterday." Then he turned to her and said, "Now take your time, honey. I'm sure the man doesn't mind the wait."

With curiosity Father Bill began, "I'm sorry to hear that. I've not been told anyone in the parish has passed. Who was it?"

"Oh," the man said, "he wasn't from your church. Oh, no. It was Wilma's father, Rudolph Meyer. He just lived out this way."

In the silence that followed, Father Bill's heart sank. He waited.

Gathering herself together, the woman wiped her eyes one more time and blew her nose before she looked straight at Father Bill. "I can't imagine why, but apparently Daddy must have made friends with you. He told us before he died there was a letter on his dresser about his final request." She handed the letter to Father Bill. "I couldn't believe it when I read it, but since that's what he wanted. I'll accept it."

With a shaky hand he took the letter to ask, "What is in this? What is this all about?"

Her husband cut in, "The letter states he wants you to officiate at his funeral. Strange, but that what it says."

Father Bill stood. "I'm so sorry you've lost your father. He was a really good friend to me. So sorry." There was a long pause before he continued. "You do realize that I can't do that. Your family is Baptist and I'm Catholic. It wouldn't be right. I doubt your minister would allow that. My church wouldn't permit burial service from our church nor allow me to officiate in the Baptist church. I'm sorry."

"We've thought about that," the man said, standing up. No. We wouldn't want him buried from your church and you say you can't come to ours to officiate."

"That's right," Father Bill said.

The woman, now feeling comfortable, stood and took Father Bill's hand. "Daddy must have really liked you. I must respect his request in some way. Could you come to our church and give the eulogy?"

With a warm, friendly smile Father Bill offered, "I'd love to do that but doubt your pastor would want a Catholic priest in his church to deliver a eulogy. They'd all know I was Catholic as my church rules say I must dress as a priest when officially taking part in any church services."

She squeezed his hand. "Oh, would you? I'll make him make you welcome. He must. I'll....I'll..."

The second morning after their meeting, arrangements was made for the funeral services. The pastor was to lead the procession, followed by Father Bill in his robes and new cowboy boots clonking up the aisle to take a seat next to the podium. Yes, there were "Ahs" and "Ohs" from the congregation.

That evening he wrote in his diary. "It was a beautiful service for my good friend, Mr. Meyer. I'll never forget looking out and seeing all the shocked, white eyeballs staring at me. Bless all of them, O' Lord and forgive Mr. Meyer his sins. May he now be home with you in heaven for all eternity."

He closed his book. With tears in his eyes he looked up. "Ruddy, together we caught fish but best of all, I caught a wonderful friend. Thanks for sharing a part of your life with me."

Chapter 3

Coming from the shed that housed an old tractor, Father Bill saw Rob Bleu was headed over to see him. Rob's stride was that of a messenger with a message.

Father Bill did purchase items at the General Store, and pick up his mail, but conversation with Rob or Emmie Lou was never more than needed to conduct the business.

Rob's voice, as usual was deep and loud, when he called, "That depends on what you want to do. Hold up there, Father. I got to ask you something. Only take a minute."

Opening the front door, Father Bill said, "Well, come on in. There's still hot coffee in the pot. I've been wanting to catch you to ask you about something."

The offer was so welcoming Rob followed him into the house, through the living room and into the kitchen.

Pouring the coffee, Father Bill asked, "How do you like it? Sugar, cream or both?"

Wishing for a laugh, Rob replied, "Strong, hot, and black."

Father Bill slid into the chair across from him. "So what brings you over?" he asked. "Not that I mind. It's always nice to have someone to talk with."

Rob often questioned why this young priest was here. Usually priests assigned to this parish were old or in bad health. They stayed to themselves and the members of their church, and were seldom seen out of the house or church. Now this guy didn't stay in the house much and was gone a lot.

He wished to get his business over with and back to the store so he began, "Well, I come over to invite you to Emmie Lou's surprise birthday party. It's gonna be down Highway PP at my sister's house. She lives in the little blue house with the red barn in back. Next Saturday at two o'clock."

"That's nice of you to ask me. I'd enjoy that."

Rob continued on, "I figured since you're Catholic and

she's Catholic, she'd be happy 'bout you being there for her birthday. The ol' gal's gonna be fifty."

"I didn't know she was Catholic."

"Yeah, she is but don't come over here very often. She was married at sixteen to some old geezer who mistreated her. She left him. I was working at the lead minds before I hurt my back. That's where we met up. We both like string music. Me and her—we fiddle pretty good too. She's better than me. So you'll come?"

"Yes. Thank you. Now I have a question. I was out there looking in that shed again. There's an old rusty tractor in it, but I can't get it started. I was wondering, if some day when you have time, if you would look at it to give me some advice on how to get it running?"

Rob's interest perked. "Is that ol' Case tractor still out there? That son-of-a-gun is from back in the thirties, I bet. They made 'em to run on diesel or kerosene back then. If'n that's what I think it is it belonged to my Grandpa Bleu."

Nodding his head yes, Father Bill said, "Could be. It's very rusty but the name Case is on it. I'm sure of that."

Rob smiled. "What do you want with it? Ol' Man Gruder cuts the grass in the yard and cemetery."

A slight embarrassment was in Father's voice when he replied, "Truth is Rob, I don't like to see anything just sitting around not being used or enjoyed. If nothing else, we could take turns riding it up and down the road."

Rob extended his hand, "How's about I come over after two or two thirty this afternoon. I can't promise you we'll get it started, but I'd sure like to give it a try."

A little after two that afternoon Rob and Father Bill disassembled the working parts of the old Case tractor to soak some parts in pans of oil, wire brushing off the rust, and wondering what could be salvaged or replaced to make the old tractor run again.

Behind the general store was a large shed where Rob stored many old items both good and junk. Occasionally he would take Father Bill back there to sort through items just for the enjoyment.

The first Sunday after her birthday party, Emmie Lou rose early to work in the store. Soon she missed Rob, who should have been helping her. First she called him, but no answer. She opened the door to a side room and he was not in there. A little later she checked to see if he was out in the shed, but he wasn't. After a while she went upstairs to look for him.

Not finding him anywhere, she began to worry.

It was near time for Mass to be over, so she went back downstairs to unlock the front door. Through the window she spied Rob. He was the first one out of church and sprinted across the road.

She stepped back with her hands on her hips to accost him when he entered. "What in the hell were you doing over there?"

Paying little mind to her anger, Rob posted himself behind the counter to wait, but said, "I just wanted to go over to see what the old boy had to say."

Still flushed, Emmie Lou came back with, "Well if that don't beat all. You laugh at me when I want to go and you snuck over there. I don't know what's happening to you."

When the last customer left, Rob locked the store door. Time allowed her blood pressure to drop and Emmie Lou asked, "Well, what did you think? You didn't say."

He faced her with his arms folded and a firm stance, "I liked what the old boy said. Kind'a thought one time he was talking right to me."

She cut in, "Well, I'll be damn, Rob. You know I needed

help and you just took off. Didn't say a word. Now what good did that do you goin' over there?"

He walked over and took her hand, "Well, I sat there thinking 'bout us when they all went up to get that bread and wine. You know—you and me—we're not gettin' any younger. Maybe we ought to start going over there every Sunday. Like them other folks do."

"You ol' fool, did you forget I was married before you. I can't go to communion."

He was confident with his answer. "He and I already talked about that. Father says you can always go and so can I. There's ways, but it takes time to like erase the first marriage when it was a bad mistake. We could git married again—right over there. That old boy is really up on the laws. It'd cost a pretty penny, but it'd be worth it."

Tears of joy rolled down her cheeks. "Rob, you'd do that? You'd really do that for me?"

He took her in his arms, "You know, I don't always show it but I do love you. We could start goin' next Sunday."

She looked up into his eyes, "You mean you would go too—every Sunday with me?"

"I'm thinkin' about possibly doing more than that. I just might start them lessons to learn to be Catholic. Been givin' it some real thought.

July 11th, Rob made his first communion along with Wilma, Rudolph Meyer's daughter, and her husband Charles Elliot. After Mass, Emmie Lou invited everyone to a brunch in their back yard. Father Bill received the most attention when he rode the newly painted, deep red Case tractor with the black seat across the road for the celebration.

Chapter 4

Every Wednesday morning after Mass, Sis Telaman and Rose Wilaberger, both in their sixties, went to the priest's house to clean and often do laundry. Father Bill always rose an hour earlier to remove any correspondence or records from the top of the desk and dining table. Twice he saw Sis taking time out to read anything that might interest her. He chose not to mention it because he appreciated their help. From his house they would go back to clean the church and they was also a dedicated committee of two, decorating the church for special days. When he offered to pay for the expenses they always refused.

Two other perks were Mr. Gruder's mowing and James and Meg Olheimer never missed a Friday to bring him fresh milk, eggs, and butter. Each explained they didn't have the monetary means to contribute a lot of money, so this was their way to give to the church.

Once they got to know him, he was showered with cookies, slices of cakes, pies and every now and then cooked meats and vegetables. Rose said, they were all thankful for a young priest who liked to eat, and country ladies usually like to cook.

Mr. Gruder made wine in a barrel from his Concord grape vines. Often he brought a bottle to share with Father Bill.

One day after Mr. Gruder left, Father Bill wandered over to the old hall. As he entered, his eyes went to the small stage. The ripped and dirt covered stage curtain barely clung to a wire. One piece was torn off and used to stuff in a broken window pane. Picnic tables were strewn about. Several of the folding chairs once stacked were lying on the floor and rusting. Sawhorses and planks were shoved to one end. A few benches were flipped sideways or upside down. Old tools lay about rather than stored for later use. A small room housed an old stove, sink, a shelf with pots and a couple of large cast-iron skillets. He doubted the wobbly, wooden kitchen table could take much weight. The only live things in view were spiders that freely placed their webs wherever they chose. Dead mice added to the unpleasant musty smell. A miniature dust storm could be made with only a slight wave of his hand.

He believed the interior walls to be solid. Outside it was obvious the brick needed to be tuck-pointed but the walls looked good. He didn't need to be in construction to know the windows and doors must be replaced. Also, the roof leaked.

That's about it, he said to himself.

A week later when Mr. Gruder stepped of the tractor to greet him, Father Bill said, "Come on up and sit a spell. Yesterday I bought a bottle of white grape wine we can try. Need to talk with you."

Sitting his glass down on the table, Mr. Gruder asked, "So what be on your mind? Somethin' 'bout my mowin'."

"Oh, no. Nothing like that. I took another look at that old hall. I like it. It could be fixed to be real functional. When I checked with the archdiocese to see about getting bids to restore it, did I get a surprise."

Mr. Gruder cut in, "Them folks ain't gonna give us no money for nuttin."

Father Bill laid his hand out on the table. "May as well tell you all of it. They said this church has been operating in the red for some time. Actually they're considering closing it. I could be the last chance it has. I'm going to do my best to not let that happen."

"Kinda spectin' it, I was. Don't know as you can do nothin'."

"You're right. I can't, but together, we can. What were the activities held in that hall when it was usable?"

Recalling those day when he was a boy, Mr. Gruder said, "Thar was weddin's, picnics, dances, political speeches, meetin's, plays, and lots of things." His face flushed red when he said, "First time I ever kissed a girl was out thar behind it. Use'ta be some bushes back down thar."

Father Bill laughed, "Now you surprise me—sneaking around kissing girls. Was that one Mrs. Gruder?"

Mr. Gruder was serious when he replied, "Oh, no. In those days you didn't kiss a girl if you were planning to marry her. No, sir. Even now Mrs. Gruder won't let me to hold her hand when we's out."

Still the story perked Father Bill's interest, "So, who was that girl?'

Shaking his head he said, "Oh, no. You kiss a girl back then and tell somebody, you never got to kiss another girl. To this day I won't tell. No, sir. I never forgot it though. She was on the way back from the outhouse and I was goin'. That's how we met up to get to talkin'."

His voice dropped in regret, "It's all gone now. Them ol' outhouses like me, about ready to fall down."

"What happened to the hall? Looks like someone just put a lock on the door and never returned."

"Well the ol' folks were gettin' too old to run things and the younglings just didn't take it up. Can't get 'em to even come to Mass anymore. Least not here."

"Okay. That's it. Let me think about it. I'm sure we could get that hall back in use. It would pay for itself and more."

The next Wednesday Father Bill asked Rose and Sis to come back to his house after they cleaned the church.

Sitting at his table with cups of coffee, he said, "We need to bring the hall back into use. Now, money is scarce or maybe none at all, but it has to be done."

When he explained his contact with the archdiocese he was expecting to see shocked faces; however, they appeared aware of the circumstances.

"Not surprised about the archdiocese," Sis up and said, "and don't think we'll get a miracle to rework that old hall. Doubt if we could get anyone interested even to tear it down."

"Now," Rose corrected, "Sis, leave Father finish talking."

"We need the community to chip in with free work and some, who are able, to make a donation for the materials. Have some fund raisers for supplies.

Sis piped up again, "Even if we could get the money, they'd take it away from us if they knew what we were doing."

"How would they know?" Rose asked.

"I know...they'd know because you'd have to get permission from them to build on their property," Sis said.

With a nod Father Bill explained, "Sis is right; however we're not building on the property. It's already there. We're only doing repairs."

"Now here's a plan that would work. All the money that's donated or earned will be handled by the co-chairmen of the project. They can open a bank account at the Salem Bank for the repairs of the building."

Sis was shaking her head no. "I'll do some of work, but I ain't being one of them co-chairmen."

Smiling, Father Bill said, "That's fine Sis. I understand. We need a lot of people working. Instead of the whole project, you could be a committee chairman for one of the projects to raise money since you know almost everyone in the area."

"Yeah, you could chair homemade items for sale," Rose said. "Even oversee a quilt raffle."

Excitement showed as Sis said, "Maybe a bake sale, too." She then turned to Rose and snapped, "And what are you going to do if I do all that?"

It was the perfect opening for Father Bill. "Rose's job will be one of the co-chairmen for the whole project. Rose you're a born leader like Sis, and you also know everyone. The other co-chairman must be a man for the labor. A young man who knows about construction would be perfect."

Sis's interest peaked, "Rose, how about Don, your son-in-law. He builds houses. Of course, he's not Catholic but your daughter is. She could make him do it."

"I don't know about that. He'd be good but as you say, he is not Catholic."

Pleased with the idea, Father Bill said, "Rose, bring him tomorrow night. Leave your daughter at home. I don't care if he's Catholic or not. I'll cool a six pack. I bet together, we could get him to listen to us."

Rose's laugh was boisterous when she said, "Beer. Good Father. That'd be better than sprinkling holy water on him. I'll do my best."

Ron and Rose arrived at the priest's home right after seven and the introductions were made.

Father Bill explained all that needed to be done, and they walked back to look at the building.

"What are you going to do with it?" Ron asked.

"Well that's up to the community. I see it as a hall for the use of the community, plus a way to make money for the church. It could be rented, used for picnics, dances, donated for a place to meet to communicate important things happening in the community, activities for the kids like scouting and Future Farmers of America. Once it's complete, I see many things happening here. Have a men's club to meet here. Not necessarily Catholic men but men from the community who would want to come. I know it needs a lot of work. A new kitchen with refrigerator and a cooler in the hall for drinks."

Ron liked what he was hearing but said, "You have any idea how long it would take me in my spare time to redo this building? Maybe if I start tomorrow it'd take me a year or more. There's a ton to be done, and I'm not a miracle worker."

"Oh, no! Father Bill said, "You're the co-chairperson working with Rose. We must get lots of volunteers to help with the work. When you show me what you need and how to do it, I'd be good help. I'd have a lot more time than most."

"You're serious aren't you?" Ron asked. "You really want to do it."

He slapped Ron on the back, "Now let's go back up to the house, get another beer and start making a list of the materials we need to get started. When do you want to start?"

Ron snickered, "You know, if you want to stop working in religion, any used car salesman would jump to hire you."

"What about the pay?" Father Bill said. He liked Ron. This gig doesn't pay much."

Chapter 5

The first church bulletin in several years was printed and available on a table in the back of the church the following Sunday. A lone article read, "Come one, come all, we're going to renovate our hall. Meet at the hall at 5:30 next Wednesday. Bring tools, as work will begin after a short meeting."

Father Bill first stood outside after the Mass to field questions. After awhile, he invited anyone interested to come back into the church for a brief meeting.

He wanted to sing out 'Glory, Glory, hallelujah', but was kept busy flinging out answers. Even Rob and Emmie Lou stayed the additional thirty-five minutes rather than immediately opening the store. Most everyone was in agreement to rebuild the hall, and wished to be involved.

Shortly before five p.m. there was a knock at his door. Opening it, a man he didn't recognize stood there, but Father Bill invited him in.

Wilbur Freeman introduced himself before he sat down. "I live off Wolfe Creek Road, and we attend the Church of Christ in Sallow. This afternoon Ron Goodman told me about how the old hall was to be renovated. That's exactly what we need here in Quaintberg."

He held out a one hundred dollar bill, and continued, "I would like to give you this to get started with the materials. It's all I had at home but I'll go to the bank this week for more. That is, if you'll accept it. I can't see why you wouldn't accept money from non-Catholics if it's for the community.

There was no hesitation in taking the money. Doing so,

Father bantered, "As far as I know money is nondenominational. The dollar is good anywhere. I sure thank you for the money and lifting my spirits."

Wilber continued, "I have just one request. I don't want anyone to know I donated any money. I'm a businessman and don't want it to look like I favor one organization. It would be impossible for me to give to everything."

"I understand. I'll tell no one. Too bad you'll not be working with the guys to rehab it. They're going to have a good time."

Wilber relaxed, "Oh, I will be. I've already taken care of that with Ron. Best I recall there's no indoor plumbing in that hall. Plumbing is my business. When it's complete, it'll have two bathrooms. I'll supply the materials at wholesale costs and my son and I will do the work for free. The labor cost is in the material cost, if anyone asks. Can you do that?"

Father Bill smiled, "Ron and Rose are the co-chairmen. I'll have to refer anyone questioning the expenses to them. That information is safe with me."

Wilber stood, "Best I be going now. You see, I have two boys to benefit from your venture. For one, we need a scout troop out here. I'll plan to be a part of that when it gets goin'."

Father Bill shook his and said, "Thank you. Now I thought of just one more thing. Hope I'm not treading too much on your generosity, but that hall could use a drinking fountain when your boys are playing outside. You need to add one to the contract. Couldn't cost much more, could it?"

Wilber grinned and said, "I was warned to watch out for you. I guess you want one inside and one outside. If that's what it takes to get the job, all right. Now I really must be going. Kate told me dinner would be ready about six. Have you eaten yet?"

"Well, no."

"How about coming home with me for dinner? We're having fried chicken and you can meet Kate. She was born Catholic, but stopped going to church after she was in her early teens."

"Did you say you were having fried chicken?" Father asked.

"Yes, sir. Sure did."

"Let me grab my jacket. Priests and preachers are alike. None of us ever turn down a fried chicken dinner."

Ron dropped by the rectory Monday night to lay out his plans. "First," he said, "the roof must be fixed to protect any work done below. Men not able to work on the roof will start clearing the hall. We'll make three stacks. One to be kept, one to be burned, and another to be hauled away. Eddie Gabel and his son will be there on Wednesday. Both have roofing experience. John Short and his brother, Tom, told me the hall must be rewired to code. They're gonna' do that. Red Stone and his son are bricklayers and will do the tuck-pointing. They can't be there until next week but want to help. Wilbur said he would talk to you about the plumbing."

Father Bill's mind was overloaded which made him speechless for few seconds. Finally the words came.

"Ron, this is wonderful, but first we must find ways to get money to buy the materials. We're starting out penniless. I do have a one hundred-dollar donation to give to you. It was given to me Sunday afternoon."

Ron was tickled to learn this. "Well, I be damned, Father. What have you been doing? I've been out talking with the boys, and already have two hundred and seventy-three dollars in donations. Just wait till Friday night when everyone gets paid. Jane is making a bunch of lotto tickets for me to raffle-off one of my Dad's old twenty-twos. Five bucks a ticket or three for ten. That'll go over well. All profit. John, Red, and I are gonna hit every bar in Jasper and Salem that night. Care to come with us?"

"Thanks, but as you know I'm not a real beer drinker. You surprise me. I can't imagine anyone else taking such interest in this project. You're doing a great job. What motivates you to do this?"

Ron shuffled from one side to the other, before he spoke in a serious tone. "Well, you see, Father, I'm not much into your religion; however, I'm not much into any other one either. I told Jane once that if I was into her religion my saint would be Saint Joseph, since he was a carpenter too. Maybe that's it."

Father Bill thought Ron did have an interest and decided to follow up on it. "That's good, Ron. Anything you want to talk about or know, I'm always available. I'm sure that made Jane's day to hear that from you. Does she encourage you much to consider coming to church?

A chuckle burst from Ron when he replied, "Oh, no. She just said, Ron, you picked Joseph because he was a carpenter. Not all carpenters are big beer drinkers. You only want to go to heaven if you can find someone to drink with."

Realizing this one was not ready, Father was amused. "I have to meet Jane. She sounds like a real jolly person."

"You will. She'll be down here telling everyone what to do when we get started. I've got several promises from guys to start Wednesday. Just hope they all show up."

As a reminder, Father said, "Don't forget. I'll be there, but you have to show me what to do and how to do it. Maybe I could begin my apprenticeship by carrying the shingles up the ladder to you."

Walking toward the kitchen, Ron said, "That, or if you have a beer in the fridge, I'll find you a softer job."

Reclining back into his chair, Father Bill called back, "Help yourself and bring me one. I want to become a good carpenter."

Wednesday morning Rose and Sis rushed to Father's house and into the kitchen. Father, pouring their coffee, sensed excitement. Before she even took a sip of the coffee, Sis rose, holding a small brown paper bag high above the table. With the top open, she turned it upside down. Dollar bills floated down, while coins dropped and rolled around. Two checks were also dumped.

"Count them, if you like," she said proudly. "There's two hundred and forty two dollars and a half. More will come."

Another surprise for him. He was cheerful when he asked, "My, my, where did you get all of that?"

"We talked to people and asked for help, Rose said. Some only had a couple of dollars. There's a check from The Sallow Funeral Parlor for a hundred dollars. We promised them a good ad every week on the back of our church bulletin for a year."

"Wait a minute," he said. "We don't have a church bulletin. That would be false advertising. We'd better return that."

Sis was quick with the response, "Oh, we will have. My niece is going to help me with that. In the beginning, I'll write it up and she'll type and run it off. We can sell more space in the future. He only bought one quarter of the page. In fact, we gave him a big discount since he was our first advertiser."

"And the other check?"

"State Farm. He was a little hesitant, but I reminded him he wasn't the only insurance company around now."

You should have heard her pitch, Father," Rose said.

"How's that?"

"At first he wasn't receptive but she spoke up and said, "You, of all people, should know about competition. You're no longer the only insurance company in town, so you better start advertising in our bulletin."

"You didn't use a gun anywhere when you were out, did you?" he teased.

They were all still laughing when Rose added, "Not yet, Father. Don't worry. I'll keep an eye on her."

Five-thirty was the start time to begin the work; however, as early as four forty-five, pickup trucks began to arrive. Each truck had tools or a box for tools in the bed as well as coolers for their drinks. While they stood around waiting, most had a beer in their hand. Some smoked, some chewed tobacco, others dipped snuff, and as Mr. Gruder would have put it, "they all jawed." The older teen boys wandered a little farther away to toss a ball around. The big joke was when Father Bill arrived wearing a work-denim shirt, carpenter's pants, a brand-new leather tool belt, and high-top safety shoes. One man found a large red handkerchief in his truck and gave it to him.

Flapping it open to tie around his head, Father said, "This must be for sweat. I'm goin' to need it." That brought roars of laughter from the guys.

Red cracked a joke, "You know if you're serious about doing this, you only have thirty days before you have to join the union. We won't work with any scab labor on this job."

Ron arrived near five with the key to unlock the door. After a short meeting everyone found something to do. Ron and four men took to the roof to strip off the old shingles and tarpaper. Father Bill joined those who chose to empty the hall.

No one took a break and by dusk over half of the wood was showing on the roof. The hall was almost empty.

A few women arrived to help, carrying light items and

sweeping when necessary.

Two women walked up to Father to introduce themselves. The large one said, "Hi, I'm Jane Goodman, Ron's wife. This is Jane, John Short's wife. Everyone calls me Big Jane and her, Little Jane. Heard a lot about you."

"And I about you," Father said.

Both Janes cackled. "Bet what we heard about you was a lot better than what you heard about us," Jane Goodman said.

He liked them right away. "I don't understand. They only talk bad about you to your faces? Behind your backs they say good things? And about me?"

The smile on Big Jane's face was ear to ear, "You know how to handle Ron. He's like Ol' Dude. Offer Ol' Dude a bone and he'll do anything. Ron'll be here 'til the beer runs out."

The last to climb down was Ron, who called everyone over. "Now I don't think it would be good to leave things go 'til next week. I'm coming back tomorrow night to work on the roof again. Anyone wishing to join me should be here at five-thirty. I was surprised to see most of the wood up there is good. Some areas will need replacing. It's gotta be completed before the next rain. "

There were several, "I'll be here," and "count me in," responses. Ed Tightzel called out, "I got some big pieces of plywood in the barn. I'll bring 'em to see if you can use 'em. Ain't doing me any good."

"I got some too," came from Eddie Gabel, "Think together, maybe that's all that'll be needed. I got nails and tar, too. Plenty to do the job."

"But where's the money for the paper and shingles?" Ed asked.

Ron was proud to announce, "We have a few hundred already donated and some money-making projects are in the works."

"Never changes," Ed said, "This church is always wantin' money, money, money."

Ron was annoyed so his voice was sharp when he said, "You can't build nothin' without materials, and nothin' is cheap. Ed, no one said you have to give."

"And no one asked me either."

Soon, the gathering broke up for the night.

About fifteen minutes after Father Bill reached his house, the door bell rang. Looking out he saw Ed's truck. It crossed his mind as he answered the door to invite him in that Ed was coming for trouble.

Ed refused to sit down saying he had to get on back to the house. "I was on the way home, but kept thinking about that ol' hall. So I turned around and came back. Here's my check for a hundred dollars. I know you're gonna come up short so thought I'd better help out. Don't know as we need that hall, but it's already started."

"Ed, didn't you ever have a good time in that hall?"

"Well, me and Anna got married here and had a party in the hall afterwards. We usta' come to dances sometimes, but times have changed. "No one wants to do a picnic or anything anymore. It's gonna look better, but doubt if it's used."

"Well, thanks anyway for the money. The hall is a blessing so it should be maintained. Thanks again for helping."

Ed, with some agreement, made his last statement. "Well, that's about it, but it makes me mad that this church always wants more money."

"Goodnight, Ed, give my best to Anna. She seems to be taking an interest in it."

"Oh, yeah. If they have a kitchen, I know she will. She's good at runnin' things like that. Always was, but she just couldn't get enough help to keep it goin'."

Father closed the door, turned off the outside lights and fell into his recliner. His tired was a good tired. He enjoyed the work and liked the guys. His intentions were to thank God in prayer for all the blessings of the day as soon as he caught just a little rest. That didn't happen. In a minute or two his eyes closed, his mouth opened and the sound of snoring filled the room.

Chapter 6

The crew restoring the hall was well ahead of schedule. In just three months the exterior was finished, except for the new addition to house a perfectly designed commercial kitchen. Inside, the bathrooms were complete and the wiring up to code. It was ready to begin the completion of the walls and ceiling. The floor, made of oak, only needed to be sanded and varnished.

The money kept coming in to meet the expenses. There were donations, but mostly it came from raffles of quilts, guns, a TV, a week in a condo at the Lake of the Ozarks, and more. Bake sales were regular after Mass each Sunday. Not only did they do bake sales, but on Saturdays they sold bakery goods in Sallow and Javelle in front of the grocery stores. Two men got together and organized four ham shoots.

The word was out that the old, historic hall in Quaintberg was being renovated. That brought cars and trucks of onlookers from as far away as Poplar Bluff and Fredricktown. Many times, attendance at Mass on Sunday more than tripled Sundays in the past. One Sunday a few stood as the pews were filled. It was a combination of those returning to the church, visitors who at one time lived in the area and the curious. Both the *Sallow* and *Javelle Times* ran articles with photos on their front pages. The general collection on Sundays increased more than the attendance, placing the church's financial status well in the black. Father Bill refused to allow a second collection for the hall, but a basket was placed near the door for donations if anyone wished to contribute. That amount was usually larger than the general collection. Twice, someone dropped a gold piece into the basket. A nursery from Poplar Bluff made contact asking for permission to landscape the area around the hall for allowing them to place a small sign in the front to advertise their business.

Good fortune fell to Rob and Emmie Lou's general store. They arranged picnic tables in Emmie Lou's rose garden and installed a deli counter to sell sandwiches and side orders on weekends. Their hours on Sundays changed to open until two in the afternoon.

Every first and third Sunday of the month, tables were placed on the church grounds to rent to vendors for craft sales and spaces for farm products to be sold. Big Jane sold tickets for people to ride the hay-wagon pulled by the Father Bill's old Case tractor down Quaintberg Road and back.

Father was in awe of the parishioners because the old and young all worked, with no one complaining about the hours. He stayed as far back from the activity as possible except occasionally dressing as a farmer in bib overalls, red shirt and straw hat to drive the tractor. He allowed no personal interviews. The *Popular Bluff Gazette* once referred to him as Rev. McHeck, the mystery priest. He was a mystery priest to outsiders, but in the church circle he was respected and loved.

The door to the church was never locked, nor was his front door. The only closed door to his house was his bedroom. Many items needed during the renovation were stored in his house and basement. Workers lightly knocked before entering or called out to let him know they were in the house. Impromptu meetings were held around his table. Before long, young families who attended Mass in Salem or Jasper were returning to St. Francis.

Many requests were made. Some wanted two Masses on Sunday, while others wanted one on Saturday night and one on Sunday.

The area, where in the beginning teenage boys only tossed a ball around, became their softball field and they wanted a backstop. If the boys were to get a backstop, the girls wanted a volleyball court. Father Bill silently wished for a tennis court or handball court, but figured that wasn't to be. Some wanted to paint the inside of the church while others wanted to totally update it. A request was made for a large St. Francis statue outside.

There were no more quilts to be raffled so the older ladies asked to use his basement to quilt new ones. That began right away on every Tuesday and Friday. Carpeting for the church was mentioned by many. There was talk of purchasing new pews or refinishing the old ones.

Father's only decision was to say no to build a cry room. He promised to speak louder, but loved to hear the cries of the young. To him, it meant that St. Francis would continue to grow.

After Mass, in early August, he asked everyone to be seated and said, "We're growing and so are our needs. It's time for St. Francis to have a church council to make the decisions as what should be done next and when."

A woman from the back called out, "We don't need a council. You're doing fine."

His face flushed as he said, "Thank you, but I'm only here as your spiritual leader. Tomorrow the Bishop could pull me out to send me somewhere else

"No" and "no way" comments drowned out his next words, so he waited until it was quiet again.

"Especially when the Archbishop finds out you built an addition onto the hall without the Archdiocese consent," he said. "When he learns about that, I may be assigned to clean toilets in St. Louis." When the laughter died he continued, "I would like six people to volunteer to serve six months on the council. They'll write the bylaws and take the responsibilities for managing the property. After six months, there'll be a general election to elect new members for the council. If I don't have volunteers I will," his finger extended out, "appoint you and you and you. Or maybe the best yet, could be the first six adults to leave today are officially our new council."

Before dark, fourteen people volunteered. He called each of them to request a meeting. At the meeting the names were placed in a box and six were drawn, although the other eight were asked to sit in when the bylaws were written.

Excitement grew because September third was the date to cut the ribbon for the renovated hall. Photographers from all around came for the ribbon cutting. Father Bill refused to cut the ribbon, insisting that Rose and Ron do the honors. He didn't wear his collar and requested the parish members only address him as Bill when in public. No one was to point him out as their priest.

After the ten o'clock Mass, a full day was scheduled. To begin, there would be a parade down Quaintberg Road and back, consisting of decorated tractors, old trucks and cars, plus kids leading their pets. Two prizes were to be awarded, one for the best decorated vehicle and the other for the funniest dressed character. Spectators lined both sides of the road to watch.

At eleven thirty, chicken or beef dinners were available in the hall. Bingo was to be played outside. Three booths would be for the children.

A beer license was acquired and would be sold. One last quilt was donated to be raffled. A softball game between the teenage boys and their dads would begin at two. Father Bill was to be the umpire.

The horseshoe tournaments were scheduled to begin at four o'clock. First to pitch would be the men aged 19 and over, second for the teenagers, and last, the ladies. A few gathered to watch until the ladies stole the show, drawing a good crowd. It was doubtful any one of them ever pitched a horseshoe before. They screamed, laughed, shouted and joked around until the game was called for time. No one got a ringer and only a few accidentally landed a horseshoe inside the box.

The reporters persisted on questioning everyone about the absence of their priest. It first annoyed them, but when the reporters kept on, they told tall stories about his unusual behavior. Some described him as elf-like, while others said he was only slightly shorter than the Alton giant. It was reported he was hairless or resembled an ape.

About twelve-thirty Father Bill stood inside the hall talking to Ron, Big Jane and Little Jane. A reporter walked over to them and said, "Your hall is nice, but I find people here to be a little strange. I've been told all kinds of stories about your McHeck priest. No one apparently knows where the priest is or seems to care."

Big Jane looked directly at him and said, "Oh, you're wrong. He's here now. I just saw him go into the men's room."

The reporter, with two others behind him, rushed over to get a picture and hoped for an interview when he came out. When John Short walked out camera lights flashed. John was confused, but no way was he going to give an interview. He rushed back into the bathroom and held the door shut for awhile. Believing the photos were the best they would get from the mystery priest, they rushed to their cars. The newspaper's next issues carried several pictures of the day, as well as one of John Short in front of the men's bathroom as Father William McHeck, the shy priest.

A country western band was hired to play from six till eight. All the chicken and beef was sold by two-thirty, allowing plenty of time to rearrange the hall for dancing that evening. Beer, soda, popcorn, and chips, were sold over the counter from the kitchen.

A good number of people stayed or returned for the dance. No sooner than the music began the floor filled with dancers. They played waltzes, two steps, polkas, and twice James Olheimer called a square dance. The young set was disappointed, so after the first break they added the Bunny Hop, Chicken Dance, Hokey Pokey, YMCA, The Twist, Cha Cha, and some swing. Three couples did the Mexican Hat Dance.

Father Bill sat with Ron and Big Jane, John Short and Little Jane, and Wilber and Kate Freehil in a far corner. Wilber and Kate loved dancing but Ron and John preferred to sit drinking their beer while Big and Little Jane danced together. The only workers needed at the time were two bartenders and two ladies to help with the popcorn, pretzels, and chips. Ed Tightzel and wife, Anna, along with their friends, Bert Steimel and wife, Jo Ann, volunteered for that.

When Father remarked, "I was surprised that Ed and Anna immediately volunteered to work during the dance. Thought they might be overly tired or wanting to dance."

"Huh," Ron said, "Ed gets free beer that way."

"Yeah," Big Jane joined in. "There go the profits from that. Watch Ol' Anna stuffing them chips down her throat. Wonder she don't choke."

"Hope she doesn't try and stuff 'em in her bra for later," Little Jane giggled.

"That's it!" John said, pulling her glass away from her. "No more beer for you. Why don't you dance with Father?"

"Come on, Father," she said, standing. "Let's cut a rug."

He first declined but everyone egged him on until he got up to dance with her.

"Just once," he said.

The band struck up *The Beer Barrel Polka* just as they reached the floor.

"Can you do that?" Jane asked.

"Can I do that?" he said, "You don't think McHeck is Chinese, do you?"

With her in his arms they began to circle the floor. Others saw them and stopped to watch. There was no doubt he was the best polka dancer in the hall and Little Jane was good. Soon they were the only couple left dancing. With loads of room, he performed every variation of the Polka he knew as the band played faster and faster. When the music stopped applause burst out. Both was sweating, but clowned and bowed this way and that. He held Little Jane's hand until they reached the table.

To Little Jane," he said, "Thank you. "John, I really enjoyed that. Thanks. Now I best be going up to the house. You better warn everyone before they leave, if anyone tells the Archbishop about that I'll have them excommunicated. "

It was a new moon and the stars were shining bright. Just before stepping onto his porch he turned. Looking up, with his arms held heavenward, he said, "Thank you, God, thank you. I have no idea what I did to deserve all these blessings. Thank you, thank you. And most of all, bless everyone in this area...Catholic and non Catholic. Amen."

Chapter 7

The church council voted to have a day just for the parish to celebrate the renovated hall on the Saturday after the opening. Kate Freehil, attending Mass again, joined Big Jane and Little Jane to make the arrangements. James Olheimer donated a pig to roast. Each family was to bring a covered dish for the celebration, plus a cake was ordered from a bakery in Sallow.

To roast the pig required an all night watch. The men were divided into two-man shifts and changed every hour through the night. Father Bill was not scheduled; however he spent several hours observing since it was all new to him.

The morning of the celebration, Big Jane was not happy that Ron Goodman's sister from Chicago, unannounced, arrived late the night before for a weekend visit.

Ron, having completed his morning shift with the pig, walked into the kitchen where Big Jane was cooking.

"Cath must be in the bathroom already," he said, "Guess I should have gone back at the hall. She'll be a long time putting on that paint and stuff to make her look more attractive. She's always been like that."

Big Jane stopped flipping the pancakes, and turned toward him. She scoffed, "Attractive! Ha. She paints up like a billboard to say, "here I am, boys.""

He shook his head. "I can't understand why you two can't be civil to each other for a couple days. I put up with your stupid brother, and he stays a full week at a time."

The conversation ended when she said, "Forget it, Ron. If she stayed a week, I'd kill her."

Everything at the hall was going fine, so the women sat down at a table to relax.

Cath, sitting next to Big Jane, poked her in the ribs with her elbow, when she said, "Oh, my God, kid, if that one's available, I may stay a week with you."

All the women turned to look at her, as Little Jane asked, "Who are you talking about?"

Making believe she was fanning herself, Cath pointed, then replied, "That one. The 'hottee' that just walked in, and headed over to talk with Ron."

"You hussy," Big Jane said, "that's our new priest."

Cath let out a big sigh. "Honey, I didn't know you Catholics had earth angels. If he makes house calls sign me up."

Big Jane was firm when she scolded, "You'd better shut up. He's Ron's friend and priests don't mess around with women. Especially your type."

At the appointed time Father Bill walked to the podium on the stage. "Morning, everyone. What a beautiful day. I know you're all eager to sample the roasted pig, and so am I. I'll make this short. Even a thank you in big capital letters isn't enough to express what in my heart I feel toward all of you for all you have done to renovate this hall. I'm as Mr. Gruder would say, proud as a peacock, and talking with you, I know you're also proud as peacocks.

"All of you gave time and money for the project; however, there are a couple of people who deserve special thanks. First is Rose. Rose Wilberger, would you please come up here?"

Applause broke out, as Rose walked up to take a position beside him.

"Rose," Father said, "as co-chairman of this project, you took full responsibility along with Ron. I don't believe there was ever a doubt in your mind that this would be accomplished, even when I sometimes questioned it. Many were the time, I heard you say to Ron or one of the other workers, "Go ahead and get it. If we must have it, we'll find some way to pay for it." You always knew who to call to do something more to make the money to pay for it. Not only did you handle the financial end, but when a chairman of a project needed another worker, it was you they called. Now thanks to you and your workers we were able to meet all the expenses with only a few pennies left in the bank."

He reached for the shelf in the podium, and pulled out a St. Francis statue to hand her. "Please accept this small token as an award. It's only bronze, when you deserve gold. I knew there were no more quilts to raffle. As hard as everyone worked, I was afraid to call anyone to take on another project to make money for this. I'd have been the first one they hung up on."

He stepped back and took a long look at her. "You and your friends are awesome," then he gave her a big hug.

Before she stepped up to the microphone to thank all those who worked with her, she thanked Father.

When she finished, Father said, "Rose, wait right here. I want to get someone else up here with you."

Next he asked Ron Goodman to join them. Ron was one who preferred to remain in the background, and embarrassment shone as he walked up. There was applause and whistles. Reaching Father's side, with his hands in his pockets, he said, "I don't know what I'm doing up here. I'm not Catholic."

Rose reached and took his hand as she hugged him.

"Ron," Father said. "Without your skills, your leadership, and good heart, I don't know where we would be today. The church is indebted to you, and so is the community. I saw this hall rehabbed to be useable, but you saw this hall to be a grand place for the community. You and your friends turned a run-down building into a beautiful landmark. I say thank you, and I know everyone here appreciates all the hours of hard labor spent to accomplish it.

"As you know Rose is tight when it comes to money. When I told her, I needed just a little for today, that's all she gave me to spend...just a little."

"Boy is that true," Ron said. "She'd say, 'Ron, before you go buy it, have you checked around to see if maybe someone has it, or something close to it you can use?' Sometimes, she was right, too."

Father continued, as he handed a box to Ron, "You both, as a team, did a wonderful job. Accept this as a token of our appreciation."

Ron flushed, "Now, Father, you shouldn't have done this." He removed the lid to find a chrome plated hammer with a St. Joseph medal welded to the end and his name engraved on the side. He took it out and held it for everyone to see. He smiled when he said, "Don't no one ask to borrow my hammer. It's too pretty to drive a nail. I'm gonna hang it on the wall. Thanks."

He shuffled from one side to the other, holding the hammer in his hand. He would look at it and then up to the audience and back at it again.

Finally he walked to the podium, and cleared his throat. "Well, I never expected nothin' like this. This's great, but I wish I had one for every guy out there. You're a great bunch of guys. I salute you." He stood for a moment as if in thought, then he called Rose to his side. Putting his arm around her, he said, "And I couldn't have had a better person to work with than this here Rose, my mother-in-law."

There was more applause, and he kept shuffling his weight from one side to the other before he began again, "Yes, we spent all the money or most all of it. And that's sad, since we didn't get an award to give to the most deserving man here. A man with a vision—and I must say, a damn good salesman too. A year ago, had you told me we were going to do this, I'd have bet you a couple hundred bucks that I was, in no way going to be doing it. He's so smooth; I don't even know when he hooked me. He's changed all of us, and made us his friends for life." Turning to Father, his voice was humble as he said, "Big Guy, we love you."

Father walked forward to extend his hand, but instead Ron grabbed him in a hug. Rose put her arms around the both of them, and the audience rose to their feet.

Standing before the microphone, Father waited for the applause to die down before he said, "Again, I thank all of you. Now I'm hungry. Let's bow our heads for prayer before we eat." He first bowed, and then looked up and said, "I'll make it short for you. No sense boring God when we've been blessed with good food to eat."

The day was filled with activities; however, three men chose to go back to the church and finish painting since the carpet was to be laid on Monday.

That afternoon, after the dads were beaten again at softball by their sons, a decision was made. Every Tuesday evening the softball field was to be for dads only to practice. The boys only agreed if, Thursday nights the field would be theirs.

It aggravated the girls that the boys got their backstop before they got their volleyball court. The council attempted to accommodate by buying two badminton sets. They used them; however, they continued to beg for the volleyball court.

Two days before, Ernest Freehil applied for St. Francis to host a Boy Scouts of America Troop and Lois Gable was in the process to apply for a Brownie Troop. James and Meg Olheimer, who loved farming, were anxious to get started with Future Farmers of America for the kids.

All those activities were the main subjects of conversation that afternoon.

Late in the afternoon Father called over John Short, Red Stone, Ed Gable, and Ron to talk about organizing a Men's Club. First, it was said that there was too much going on, so there would be no time for it.

Father explained that many things were now off the table. No longer would there be craft shows and produce sold on church property. The hall was complete. James and Meg Olheimer, whose home was located on Highway PP, planned to start a farmer's market every weekend during the summer. Emmie Lou wanted the craft shows to continue, plus to add antiques and used items to be sold. She and Rob laid out an area to rent spaces next to their store.

Red Stone agreed to be the leader in organizing the men's club.

Mr. Gruder, hearing of the little cottage businesses, wanted to sell his homemade wine. He was told there were a lot of legal matters to be done before he could, which didn't make him happy. "Dad-danged government," he said, "Jus' wanta get their hands in everythin'. Now I ain't smart enough to get all dem things figured out on my own."

Frank Talaman, Sis's husband, retired, heard of it, and approached Mr. Gruder. That afternoon, he announced negotiations were complete. He and Mr. Gruder would be partners to make and sell wine. If all went as planned, late next spring, Quaintberg would have a winery.

Father Bill got a kick out of the remarks Mr. Gruder made in one of the negotiation sessions. Mr. Gruder said, "Nows I knows a lot about dem different drinkers. Been around where they sells that stuff, lots when I's young. Dem beer drinkers, you gotta watch, 'cause when dems gets too much, dems wanta fight. Dem winos, they don't fight. Dems wanta make love."

Another change was occurring in Quaintberg. Wilma and Charles Elliot were subdividing the old Rudolph Meyer farm into parcels of three to six acres, and two new houses were in the process of being built. It was renamed Quaintberg Farm Estates.

That night, Father Bill was having a hard time falling asleep. He laid awake recalling all the changes, plus wondering what else should or could be done.

It was as if someone said to him, "There is no school-of-religion for the children." He tossed the cover back and jumped out of bed to get to the phone.

When he turned on the light, and saw the clock, he realized it was ten minutes to eleven.

He held the receiver in his hand awhile before placing it back in its cradle.

Low, but aloud he said, "It will just have to wait till tomorrow."

Chapter 8

After Mass, Father Bill rushed to the house to change clothes knowing there were a few ladies down at the hall, decorating it for a surprise birthday party for Rose. He wanted to snare two of them to be teachers for a new religion school.

He opened the door, walked in, and called, "Is there any coffee?"

Big Jane was holding a streamer for Little Jane to tape to the wall. She called back over her shoulder, "Yeah, but you have to get your own. We're all busy."

He found a cup and the coffee. For a short time, he sat quietly watching Big and Little Jane put white paper tablecloths on the tables. Kate and Lori were arranging artificial flowers in small vases to place in the center of each.

His coffee half-finished, he spoke, "How about you ladies taking a break? I need to talk with you."

Cups filled with coffee, the four ladies sat down to see what Father wanted. He announced, "We need a religion school for the students who attend public school. Maybe we could have one class for the children to prepare for their First Communion and another for those who have made their First Communion to prepare for Confirmation. Later, a third could be a Bible study for the older teens. In the future, I think, a Bible study class for adults would be possible."

Big Jane laughed, "Father, you don't want me. I can't even teach that darn Jack, little Josh, or good ol' Ron to pick up their clothes, and take them to the laundry area. After I throw one of my fits, for a few days, they kick 'em under the beds, thinking I won't look there. Not me! I wish I had a girl."

47

Little Jane jumped right in. "I can help you with that. You can have my Melissa; however, you have to take my David too. They come as a set."

"Ah," Big Jane said, "How about a trade? We just switch. A boy and a girl get along a lot better than two boys."

"Oh, yeah," Little Jane cried, "Just this morning they were fighting again. Of course, John's usually at fault. Melissa has him wrapped around her finger. David wanted a new baseball glove. John told him he would have to wait because it's not in the budget this month. Melissa saw a sweater in Hattie's Dress Shop, and John said she could get it Saturday. David jumped up, and said, 'It's Daddy's little princess who gets everything. Daddy's jackass gets nothing,' and left the room. John just sat there and laughed."

Kate stood to go back to work, "Father, you picked the wrong group this time. Lori and I both have our hands full with our teens. Not now. We don't need to be taking care of someone else's kids."

Lori agreed, "She's right. Sorry, Father."

"Well," he said. "Have you any idea who I might get?"

As Little Jane rose, she said, "How about Anna? She likes bossing everyone around. Guess that's because she's married to Ed. Maybe she'd like more bossing time away from him to teach the kids."

Big Jane was jovial when she said, "Lucky he didn't marry me. We'd both be black and blue, all the time, if I didn't kill him. No, she's not a good selection. It'd take two truant officers to keep the kids in school with her mouth."

Kate joined by saying, "How about that new couple, the Enstruckees? Wasn't she a school teacher once?"

Agreeing, Little Jane said, "Yes, you're right. Ruth...Ruth Enstruckee. She seems really nice, and no kids yet."

48

Kate nodded, "She is nice. I like her. Tell you what, Father; if she would take charge, then to get it started, I'd be willing to help her. When it's up and going, I'm sure, there'll be others interested in helping."

They overheard Big Jane laughing with Little Jane as they walked away. "Wait til she gets my darn Jack and little Josh in her class. That'll definitely be birth control. She'll never want kids."

Father just smiled and stood. "I best be going to see her. Thanks for the coffee and the company. I'll let you know, Kate."

As he stopped in front of the Enstruckee's new home, he realized not only was the church growing, but so was Quaintberg.

Ruth Enstruckee met him at the door and welcomed him in. George, her husband, sat his briefcase down on the floor and joined them. Prior to the doorbell ringing, he was preparing to go to Javelle to check on available office space to begin his CPA firm.

Although Ruth Enstruckee taught school for two years, she was to work two or three days a week for him, until he could hire an administrative assistant full-time.

After making an apology for dropping by unannounced, Father explained why he was there.

In no time, George realized Ruth was pleased to be asked, and would definitely accept the offer. He reached down with his hand to find his briefcase before he said, "Father, if you'll excuse me, I need to be going. Ruth would be a good leader to start the school." As he turned to Ruth, he said, "Honey, it'll give you a heads-up to be a part of the community...to get to know everyone. Father has good judgment. You're perfect for it." He shook Father's hand before he kissed Ruth goodbye.

Ruth wanted to get right to work, and stated, "I'll need some instruction as this is new to me, and I suspect, quite different than teaching in public school. Do we have enough books to begin and what else is available?"

Father fessed up, "That's the problem. We're starting very near ground-zero. When I came here, I only found instruction for adults to be baptized. Maybe there never was anything more. We'll have to order all the material from the Archdiocese.

"So we have some background, I'll give a call to Father Morris at Sacred Heart in Javelle. He may have someone who is experienced to help us get off the ground. They have a school from kindergarten through the eighth grade. They even have a couple of semi-retired nuns teaching, so I understand."

Not deterred, Ruth grinned, "Maybe, that's not bad. Since, possibly, there never was a religion school here; they'll have nothing for comparison. When do we start?"

He was elated with his catch, but recalled Mr. Meyer's advice about fishing, 'When you got the big one hooked, reel her in slow, so you don't lose her.' "First, I'll call Father Morris to see who he may have to help us. Then I'll get back with you." Offering his hand to shake, he said, "Thanks. You've made my day."

Back at the house, he gave a call to Father Morris. Father Morris was cooperative. He promised to ask the sisters at Sacred Heart if they would be interested in helping begin a religion school at St. Francis in Quaintberg.

The phone rang, disturbing his occasional afternoon nap. "Hello. This is Father Bill. How may I help you?"

A husky woman's voice clamored, "Help me, you say? I understand you're looking for someone to help you. Now, exactly what is it you need help with?"

"Who is this? This is St. Francis Rectory?"

Her voice was lighter, almost laughing when she replied, "Yes, I know. You're speaking with Sister Jesselee Joanette Neidenhauser, but just call me Sister JJ. Everyone else does. Saves time. Father Morris told me, you don't know how to begin a religion school for children attending public schools. I think, he thinks you're a little wet behind the ears. Don't let him bother you. He's so dry behind his ears, they're beginning to crack. I've been reading, and hear a lot about what you're doing out there. I like that."

Now Father was smiling, "Well, Sister JJ, it sounds like you're the answer to my prayers."

He could hear the pride in her voice, but also laughter. "Better not count your blessing yet," she said. "We haven't met.

"This ol' gal's been around a long time so toughen up. I'll work with those who work for themselves. No 'sluffing' off or I'll quit. Don't have that many years left, and don't care to waste 'em. I spent forty years working in hospitals. Now I'm semi-retired and teaching. If you wish, Sister Hope and I could meet with you. Sister Hope, you'll like. She's seventy-six, but sharp as a tack. Not like me...she has patience. She should've been called Sister Patience. Me, the kids were probably right. If I hadn't been a nun, I'd have been a dandy army drill sergeant. I give orders and expect performance. When and where do you want to meet?"

His thoughts were running fast but not fast enough for Sister JJ. "Well, young man, speak up. Times wasting. As Mae West once said, 'My place or yours?'"

He burst into laughter. "Sister JJ, have you ever been to Quaintberg? It's just a few miles from Javelle."

Her response was sincere when she said, "Had no reason, but if you like Sister Hope and I can take a ride out there. Maybe it would be enjoyable since I'm an ol' country gal, born and raised in Louisiana. First time I went squirrel hunting with my Daddy, I was only eight years old. By the time I was ten I could hit a black-eye pea on a fence post at twenty-five feet with my Daddy's ol' twenty-two."

Now he was really laughing. "How did you get from that to becoming a nun?"

"I always knew I had the calling early on. I did, but I know there were times when Mother Superior had doubts. I was good with the gun, but not the needle. Mother Superior made everyone of us sew at least one habit for ourselves. The others were finished long before me. For me it was rip and sew...rip and sew, until finally she said, 'All right, Jesselee Joanettee, I'll accept this, so we can move on. Jesselee Joanette Neidenhauser, you'd better take my advice, work hard to learn to get assigned where they'll furnish your clothing. I always have."

It was love on the phone for him. Attempting to sound country he said, "Well, Jesselee Joanette Neidenhauser, jus' git yourself on out here, or if 'n you'd like I'd can come carry you out. 'Spect I gotta a neighbor 'round who might jes' lend you a gun. Maybe one who'd take you squirrel huntin' again."

Now she was cheerful and said, "No, that won't be necessary. If not a nun and not an army drill sergeant, I'd mostly been a race-car driver. Sometimes when I'm in the open, I like slamming the pedal to the metal. What time is Mass next Wednesday?

"Eight o'clock."

Her demeanor turned serious as she said, "Fine. We'll be there."

He was pleased. "I've a lady, Ruth Enstruckee, who will be in charge of the school. I'd like for you to meet with her...here at my house. We'll have breakfast after we meet."

"Both you and she write down the questions you have, so as not to forget anything when we meet," she said. Sister Hope and I'll be looking forward to meeting with you and Mrs. Enstruckee."

"Great," he said, and then added, "Sister JJ, there're lots of bad curves between Jasper and Quaintberg, so watch them." Back attempting to sound country again, he continued, "Now ya'll be sure and keep the metal side up and the rubber side down. Ya hear?"

Right after Mass, Sister JJ, Sister Hope, and Ruth Enstrucke joined Father at his kitchen table. It was quick to see that the nuns and Ruth was a perfect match. They liked Ruth's interest to start a religion school. Ruth was happy to get all her questions answered and more. To begin, Sacred Heart just received new books for the study in both First Communion and Confirmation. The old ones would be available for St. Francis if they chose to use them. They promised to make copies of materials they owned, which included instructions for new lay-teachers.

Toward the end of the meeting, Father excused himself and walked across the road to the General Store. Emmie Lou was ready for him, handing him his order of fresh, range-free, scrambled chicken eggs, homemade biscuits, spiced country gravy, real country-cured ham, hardwood smoked bacon, fried potatoes seasoned with tiny onion bits, and delicious fried apples.

Ruth knew his plans, so she set the table for his return.

The grins on the sisters' faces showed their surprise as Ruth and Father placed the food in bowls and on a platter to be served.

Sister Hope, with her head held high to sniff the pleasant aroma, said, "This may be my last meal, but I don't care. I'll pass with a full stomach."

Sister JJ, nudged Sister Hope, "Go ahead and eat all you want. Real country food don't hurt anyone. Put some meat on those bones. It'll be good for you. Look at me. I grew up on cornpone, hog jowl, fried potatoes, and tons of fish. All fried. My Mother, God love her, she fried everything. All she knew to do with the oven was bake bread. Never in my life has anyone ever said to me, JJ you need to put some meat on those bones. I could hibernate for two winters." Waving a biscuit in the air, she turned to Father, "You sure know what bait to use to bring us back. These are browned with heaps of butter on top."

They remained at the table enjoying each others' company for over an hour. The scrumptious fried apples were the first to go. Sister JJ ate the last biscuit with left-over gravy, while Sister Hope picked until she finished off the country ham. After being assigned to a country parish, Father's choice of meat for breakfast was always bacon, bacon, and more of that tasty, hardwood smoked bacon.

Ruth rose to clear the table. Sister JJ jumped up, ran to the sink, pushed up her sleeves and ordered, "Ruth, you carry them over, I'll wash them. Father you should know where they belong, so you dry."

Sister Hope asked, "And what about me? What duty do you have for me?"

Sister JJ chuckled, "Find a broom and sweep around the table. I'm going to let you off easy this time...no mopping."

Ruth, bringing plates to the sink, was within reach of Sister JJ's hand when she started to say, "You're our—"

Sister JJ's hand lightly went right up to Ruth's mouth, "In our Order, we're not allowed to be pampered. We're accustomed to work. But help me watch Father. Men are not the best to help in a kitchen."

Ruth left first, and Sister Hope complained of a light headache. Sister JJ suggested she take a pill and lie down for awhile. Father was most willing to show Sister JJ the renovated hall and grounds while Sister Hope rested.

Before going into the hall, they walked completely around it. Sister JJ said, "The grounds are beautiful. Must admit, it's far better landscaped than ours. Most of the time, you just see overgrown evergreen shrubs and bushes. Here's color with all the beautiful flowers, but a lot to take care of. The landscaping around the hall and church...it's all just like a magazine. You've done a great job."

He smiled, "This time you're definitely wrong. I never turned over any dirt. A landscape company from Poplar Bluff did the basics. A group of ladies got together and planted all the flowers. It's collections from their yards. I don't even water. They do all that. Isn't it beautiful?"

"I liked your church too. Well done...a blend of country and modern. You should be proud of your work."

Shaking his head, he said, "Sister, again, I did nothing or almost nothing. I give them an idea as to what could be done. They grabbed it and ran. My flock is awesome. Wait until you see the inside of the hall. Quaint on the outside, but all of today's conveniences inside. I'm blessed to be their pastor."

As they came out of the hall, he took her by the arm, "Care to walk back to our baseball field and up to the shed? There you'll see about all I've done, and not a lot of that. Rob Bleu helped me restore an old Case tractor."

"Then you cut the grass?" she asked.

"No, again. I'm not allowed to do that. Mr. Gruder does it. Has for years. He made claim to that long before I came."

From the shed, they cut back to the road, so he could take her to the General Store.

Sister JJ told Emmie Lou how much she enjoyed the food, the visit to Quaintberg, and promised to come back.

As they walked back across the street, he spied a brand new, shiny penny lying in the dirt, and said, "Lucky guy I am. Even found a new penny," and he reached down to pick it up. Before his hand reached it, Sister JJ's big, size 10 double wide, black shoe stomped down on it almost catching his fingers.

Surprised, he looked her, and claimed, "I saw it first."

"So you did," she said, "but you aren't picking it up. It's tails up. Tails up is bad luck."

"Bad luck. That's superstitious," he stated. "You're a nun."

Shaking her head, she said, "Don't matter. I was born and raised in Louisiana. Leave it. Now get on across the road. I best be getting Sister Hope back to Javelle. See them hills over there—rising to the West? Next time I'm out here I'm going to hike over to them and back."

"So, you're coming back?" he asked.

She nodded. "You can bet your boots on that. I like that Ruth. I'll be back to see if she needs any help. You should be proud of her. And I want another breakfast like we had this morning. The only thing I'd change would be to have squirrel gravy. Bet you skinny, city boys didn't know they're good to eat. They make the best gravy you ever ate."

"Right," he replied, "We city boys call 'em long, fuzzy tail rats. They're destructive."

He held the car door for Sister Hope, and stood to watch and wave goodbye. With Sister JJ at the wheel, the car, instead of peeling rubber, dug holes in the dirt forming a cloud of dust and disappeared into it. He was covered with dirt, but stood for awhile smiling from ear to ear.

First he started for the house, but turned and went across the street to find the penny. It shined bright in the sun until he took the heel of his shoe and pressed down as hard as he could. Next, with the toe of his shoe, he kicked dust over it until it was well covered.

Walking back across the street without crossing himself, he talked to God as he often did. "Dear God. I don't think I'm superstitious, but just in case Sister JJ knows something I don't, I don't wish anyone bad luck. Bless them, and thank you for all the many, many blessings I've received."

Chapter 9

The church and hall were complete. Father missed all the people working about the grounds and using his house. Now, only Rose and Sis came on Wednesdays to help with the housework. Mr. Gruder mowed the grass every Friday. Mondays, Tuesdays and Thursdays were open and lonesome for him.

He tried reading, but learned you can't read all the time. Once his eyes tired he laid the book on the cocktail table to relax. He folded his hands, intertwining them on his stomach. Moving his fingers around he didn't like what he felt.

"Wow!" he said aloud. "Son, you're getting flabby." He sat up straight to confirm his suspicions. "Yes, it's true," and then he laughed. "You're sliding into just what you said you would never become as a priest...fat and now you are talking to yourself."

Dressed for exercise, with tennis balls and racket in the trunk of his car, he drove to the community park in Javelle. After jogging twice around the one mile track he spied a handball court and made the decision to use it to practice tennis.

He was almost to the gate when a male voice called, "Hey, feller. If you like tennis, how about playing with me? I'm not really good, but like to play. Being new in town, I don't know a soul who plays."

Turning around, he saw a tall, athletic, blond, young man near his age, and walked toward him with extended hand.

"That would be fine. I'm Bill McHeck. I'm kinda in the same boat. First time I was here."

The guy shook his hand, and replied, "Please to meet you. I'm Derek Dejesus. Originally from Memphis. My first time too."

Keeping in step with him toward the tennis court, Father said, "St. Louis. St. Louis, Missouri, was my hometown."

Completing the second set of tennis, Father suggested lunch unless Derek had other plans.

Derek was quick to reply, "That'd be fine. Where do you usually eat?"

"Well, my personal favorite is Happy Time." Father said. "They have a good selection for lunch. I'll drive if you like."

Heading toward Father's car, Derick replied, "Fine with me. You didn't say what you do for a living. I'm the new pastor at Javelle Baptist Church."

Father grinned, "What a perfect set we are...kinda like salt and pepper. I'm the pastor at St. Francis of Assisi Catholic Church in Quaintberg. My first assignment. Do you have children?"

Derek laughed, "Sure hope not. I'm not married. I was engaged, but my girlfriend said if I took this job in Javelle it was over."

"Oh, I'm sorry," Father said.

Hands open out from his sides, Derek stated, "It's okay with me. It was best I learned she loves city life better than me before we married. My family was more upset when she gave me the ring back than me. Actually, I was happy it was over."

Father was driving toward Happy Time when he questioned his decision. He turned to Derek, "Being raised Catholic, attending Catholic Schools and living in a predominantly Catholic neighborhood, I'm not versed on your beliefs. Happy Time is a bar and grill. There are a couple other good places to eat."

Derek turned to him to ask, "What's wrong with Happy Time?"

Father's voice was weak with embarrassment as he attempted to explain, "They do have a good grill, but it's also a bar where they serve both beer and mixed drinks. You being a Baptist preacher, I thought maybe it may not be a place you would care to patronize."

Derek laughed, "Come on, Bill. I bet you've heard a lot of stories about Baptists and drinking, to think that. If God would have never associated with sinners, he couldn't have saved anyone. That's my thinking. Happy Times, here we come. I'm hungry for a real big, juicy hamburger."

That said, they high-fived.

Ron Goodman and John Short saw the two enter. Ron called the waitress over, "That's Father Bill, the dark headed one. Find out what he and the other gent are drinking. I'll buy them a drink."

When the waitress asked what they wanted to drink, plus told them that Ron was paying, Father waved to Ron and said, "My usual. One glass of concord grape wine, room temperature." Then he turned to Derek.

Derek smiled. "I'll be having the same, thank you."

Father was shocked, "You're Baptist and you're going to drink a glass of wine. I've always heard that was a big NO."

Derek grinned with confidence, "Come on, fellow. Jesus turned water into wine. It's in the Bible. Can't believe that's a lie. True, many Baptists don't drink, unless they're like my ol' granny. She always said, "Wine was good for thy stomach's sake." That justified her nipping a little now and then. Of course, you can overdo anything. Overdoing would be a sin. Bill, I don't know who's going to learn the most from our association. I know some about your church, but not a lot."

"If that's your interest," Father said, "you may be hanging with the wrong guy. I'm still learning myself."

When they returned to the park, they exchanged phone numbers and agreed to meet again the next Thursday to play tennis and have lunch.

Their friendship grew each week. Sometimes they drove to Sallow or Poplar Bluff to shop, see a show or watch a sporting event. They could talk with each other about anything, but the unspoken law was never to discuss religion.

One Sunday night, Derek called Father to cancel a trip to Poplar Bluff saying, he had personal business and would call after things settled. His voice was so sober; Father knew their friendship was on hold.

Three weeks went by before Father heard from Derek again. Derek's voice, over the phone, was cheerful when he asked if could he come out and talk with him. Father was thrilled to hear from his friend again, and suggested he come right away.

Fifteen minutes went by before Derek pocketed the car-keys and rushed toward Father's door. Father met him on the sidewalk, holding a pitcher of sweetened tea and two glasses. They embraced in an awkward hug instead of a traditional hand shake, and Father said, "The weather is beautiful. Thought we might walk down to the picnic area. Grab that bag of cookies—there on the porch."

It was small talk until the tea was poured, and they were comfortable. Derek turned to sit directly and face Father before he began. "I need to tell you what I came to talk about, so you hear it from me, and not from someone else. I'm having problems with my church. The deacons and I aren't a match. They may be considering canceling my contract."

Father responded, "I'm not sure of the legalities for that. Can they actually do it?"

Derek said firmly, "Yes and no. They would have to propose it to the members for a vote. I think the members may follow their recommendation."

Not certain what to say, Father asked, "Are you having a problem with the members?"

Derek smiled, "Yes, them too. We differ on several things. Truth is, I don't really care. I'd like to just walk away right now. Get it over with."

Father could think of nothing to help his friend, so he asked, "What would you do? There must be other churches in larger towns or cities who would like to have you. You should start looking." He then laughed, "I'd be glad to give you a reference, but I doubt coming from a Catholic Priest it would help."

"I'm making plans to do something else. The reason I've not been meeting with you, is I've been attending a real estate school in Poplar Bluff. I'm going to start selling real restate part-time. Next Thursday I'll go to Jefferson City for the exam to get my license."

The surprise was great, and Father said, "Wow! That's a big switch. I'm a little confused. All of a sudden, after all your education, you no longer wish to be a minister to the people? How did this come about? I'd like to be your friend and help, but I don't know enough to tell you anything."

Derek's head dropped down, "I'm not or wasn't the strong guy you may have thought I was. Most of my life, I've been letting everyone else tell me what to do. My father is a preacher, my grandfather was a preacher, my older sister married a preacher and even she's an ordained minister for youths. I was always told I was to be a preacher. It's just not for me. I know it now. It'll be a great disappointment to them, but I've made the decision to do as I want...not what they want for me."

His statement made, Derek waited to hear from Father.

Father took a deep breath and exhaled. He hoped God would come through and guide him to say the right thing. He knew he had to say something. "I can't combat that, but never lose your trust in God. Keep your faith...above all things.

"The road you're choosing will be rough for some time, but think of all the things you can do with your education to continue to serve God. A pastor has an upfront seat to serve, but as a layman, his light can shine through you as well. I believe we all have a purpose for being here at this time. Possibly for you, it's to help people find the right kind of shelter. I respect your stepping out, and pray you will find your reason for being here soon."

Derek sighed with relief. "I just hope my family sees it as you do. I needed this talk. No, I'd never lose faith. I've always been blessed. I know I have an obligation to help others."

Now they were back on the same playing ground. Father said, "I'm honored that you came to me. It shows our friendship is strong. In many ways our backgrounds are similar, yet different in others. For many years you were comfortable believing to follow in their footsteps was good for you, and you worked hard to become a top-notch preacher. Me? I never gave it a thought as a kid. As I recall, it was only my grandmother who only once ever suggested I should become a priest. I ignored her, and I was a pretty wild kid. My thoughts were, I'd more likely become a gangster than a priest...especially one, away out in the country. Then BAM! In my senior year of high school I had the calling. My skin was so tough and head so hard, it took more than one calling before I surrendered. Even in the seminary, sometimes I had doubts. Has my life changed? Sure, but I wouldn't trade places with Rockefeller."

Derek stood up. "I feel much better. So good, in fact, I bet I can beat you at tennis—right now! Think we could get a court?"

Father jumped to his feet. "Let me run get my racket. I think my purpose in life right now is to beat you...and badly today."

Derek called after him, "Oh, yeah! I hope we can get a court, so I can prove you wrong. When I get rich selling real estate, I'll buy us a membership in Sallow Country Club."

Father stopped and looked back to ask, "So you plan on sticking around here?"

"It looks that way. Wait until you meet this wonderful girl I'm dating. She said her brother lives out this way."

A month went by before Derek announced he and the Jasper Baptist Church had split. He became a full time real estate salesperson for Ira E. Berry in Poplar Bluff and relocated there.

With Derek gone, Father still went to Jasper to jog and bought exercise equipment for the basement. Before Mass each day he liked to sit on the porch swing and listen to Quaintberg, a once quiet place. Now the hammers banged like mighty woodpeckers. U.S. Postal Service once considered closing the post office was building a small building on Highway PP to house a new one.

Rob and Emmie Lou contracted to have a small house built next to the general store and rent the apartment above it. The wine tasting room was almost complete on Mr. Gruder's property. The Short brothers purchased one acre from Mr. Gruder to build two small building to lease. One was to be a barber shop and the other a beauty shop. There were always one or two houses under construction in Quaintberg Farm Estates. Someone was building some duplexes about a mile from Quaintberg Road and Highway PP. Two were already occupied. Next to that was a building under construction for a new church, The Assembly of God.

The parish continued to grow, and he believed the religion school for those to make First Communion and Confirmation was off to a good start with fine attendance. Two other women in the parish volunteered to help Ruth and Kate as their assistants. It was a surprise to him to learn from Kate that the class for Confirmation was not going as well as desired. She reported the children were not taking as much interest as she would like, and asked if he had any suggestions.

He gave it some thought before he replied.

A week later, after class, he asked Ruth, Kate, and the two assistants to join him at his table. He said, "Kate approached me about getting the children who are preparing for Confirmation more interested in learning. I, being a sports-nut, like competition. What if you divide the class into two groups? At that age I'd put the boys in one and girls in another. Once a month, hold a quiz contest and offer a price to the winners. It could be as simple as the losers must serve the winners ice cream and sit to watch while they eat it."

It proved to be very successful, and Father was satisfied; however, nothing was yet planned for the teens after Confirmation.

Early one evening Father's phone rang. The voice on the other end said, "Hey, Buddy, this is Derek. Janet and I are here visiting with her brother, George Enstrucke. If you have time, I'd like to talk with you."

Father was happy. "I heard from Ruth you were dating her sister-in-law. I was wondering if I'd ever hear from you again. Get on up here!"

The only response was a click on the phone. Within a few minutes Derek was in Father's living room. Father said, "Well, Ol' Buddy, good to see you again. I don't know what you've been doing, but from the expression on your face, it's certainly agreeing with you."

Derek's smile was a million dollar smile. "Love working with Ira E. Berry Realty, but that's not the best thing that's happened to me. I knew when I first saw Janet walk into the restaurant...she was it. No question. I learned later she felt the same way the first time she saw me."

He was so happy, tears of joy welled in his eyes. "I proposed last Saturday, and she said yes. We came out here to tell her brother and you. There was just one thing she demanded. That is, we must get married in the Catholic Church, and our children be raised Catholic. I agreed to that. We'll be married at St. John the Baptist in Poplar Bluff after my condition is met. She's willing to wait. You'd better sit back when I tell you about it. If I'm to be married in the Catholic Church and my children raised Catholic, then I want to be Catholic. That's your job to make me Catholic. Whatever it takes, I'll drive out here for it."

Father stood. He too was joyful with tears in his eyes as he moved to hug his friend. "Derek, if you're sure about this...if you can't make it out here all the time for the instructions, I'll come to you."

Derek was baptized two weeks before their beautiful wedding at St. John the Baptist in Poplar Bluff. The priest from

St. John's, at the request of Derek, invited Father Bill to assist during the wedding ceremony.

A week later, after the religion school let out, Ruth approached Father. "Father, do I have good news. George is so happy and so am I. Last night Janet told George, on the phone, she and Derek are going to be looking for property near us to make their home. There's a new house for sale in the Quaintberg Farms Estates Subdivision. It may be perfect for them."

Father smiled at the good fortune and said, "It's perfect for us too. You and I both talked about needing someone to lead a Bible study for the older children and adults. Soon we'll be able to lure Derek into it. How perfect can that be?"

Chapter 10

Although the religion school was doing well, Father thought a visit from Sister Hope and Sister JJ would be good. He called Sacred Heart Rectory to speak with Father Morris.

Father Morris's old housekeeper answered and told him 'Father Morris is at the monthly lunch with some other ministers from Jasper. Father Bill asked about the sisters, and was told, "They, too, were gone for the summer."

"Please have Father Morris to call me when he returns." he said.

Father Morris did return the call, and corrected the information. He had gone to Sallow to lunch with an old friend. The Ministers' Alliance Luncheon would be the next day, and he invited Father Bill to attend. They were to meet at Maynard's Cafe on Main Street at eleven-thirty in Javelle.

To meet with ministers from other religions and Father Morris for the first time troubled Father Bill. He thought it must be the way a girl feels on a first date not knowing what to wear. He hung the slacks and shirts he considered wearing back in the closet. His decision was to be himself and to dress similar to the average country guys he knew. He slipped on a clean, white t-shirt and slid back into the jeans he took from the drawer that morning.

He entered Maynard's Cafe, and almost bumped into a young, pretty, blond waitress. She made a fast appraisal and gave him a big, friendly smile, before she asked, "Can I help you, honey? Will others be joining you or are you alone?"

Her brazen approach embarrassed him slightly, but he said, "I'm to meet with other ministers."

She was quick to say, "Oh, you must be new in town. Follow me, honey, I think they're all here. I was on my way to take their orders." She handed him a menu and said, "The special today is chicken-fried steak. There are two nice size steaks on the plate. Bet you'd like that. That t-shirt says you're a guy who eats a lot of protein. Which church do you attend?"

He laughed to himself when he replied, "I'm the priest at St. Francis in Quaintberg."

Her hand went to her mouth in shock, "Oh, I'm sorry. I didn't know. You're a priest? I'm sorry."

His was a kind smile when he said, "Sorry? It's my fault. I should have worn my collar."

When she opened the door to the private dining room, he was the one embarrassed. Father Morris was in a black suit with a black shirt and the white collar. The others were all dressed in suits and ties. He would bet he was the only one under the age of forty-five.

The waitress walked behind the only empty chair. She pulled it back and said, "Honey, come over here." Again her hand went to her mouth, but she continued, "Oh, I'm sorry." She sensed he was new to the group, and freely made the introduction, "Gentlemen, I suspect from the expressions on your faces you've not met this gentleman. This is the Catholic Priest from Quaintberg. I didn't catch your name."

As he sat down he smiled first at her and toward them. "Bill McHeck. I'm pleased to become acquainted with you. Father Morris told me yesterday about you gentlemen getting together once a month. Seems like a great idea."

The men to his left and right reached to shake his hand and introduce themselves. Father Morris sat at the end of the table barely nodding in his direction.

It was not a surprise to him that most were knowledgeable about the changes in Quaintberg and quizzed him. The Church of Christ minister, second from his right, in a joking manner, leaned across to say, "Better keep a close eye on him. He stole a couple of my members—the Freehils. Good folks, aren't they, Bill?"

He was at ease and said, "I just took Wilber. Kate was only on loan to you. You bet they're fine people. Wilber's the new Scout Master out there. He's good on first-base too. You should come out and watch him play some Tuesday night."

The Methodist Preacher, sitting next to him asked, "You have a ball team? Why don't they join our league?"

Father Morris spoke for the first time, "That parish is too small to have a team to play in our league."

Hoping the anger didn't show, Father Bill asked, "Is it an adult or boys league? We have both teams and they're good. Not all the men playing are Catholic, but I don't suspect that would make a difference."

The Lutheran Minister handed him a business card. "Here, this is my phone number. I'm the chairperson for the league. If you like, give me a call. There's still time to pencil you in. I'd be glad to meet with you and your players. Summer season starts in two weeks."

On the way out he saw the waitress and handed her a tip.

Her face flushed a little when she said, "I'm really sorry. I should be more careful. I sometimes forget and call everyone honey. I think maybe you're right. You might want to wear that collar. Don't think most people would take you for a priest...you so young and all. You sure got me."

He laughed, "Thanks for the compliment...I guess. Your service was good. I'll be back next month. If you haven't been to Quaintberg in awhile, you should come out to the craft show and farmers market to shop on the weekends. We now have a winery. Plus, the deli at the General Store is real good. Bring your friends, too."

On the return to the rectory the remark from Father Morris kept playing on his mind. He liked his flock and would stand with them against any odds. All they needed was a good coach. He was certain there were enough big, strong, athletic men in the Men's Club to form a competitive team...a darn good team. When he thought about the teenage boys, he wasn't so sure. They had everything but a good pitcher. He recalled watching their games and he smiled as he thought, why shouldn't they be good outfielders and basemen, since they're getting a lot of practice? Even the worst batter could get a single base from their best pitcher.

He parked as close to his front door as possible, since he had a need to go to the bathroom.

When he came out of the bathroom, he saw that young teenage boy again through the bedroom window, walking around down at the ball field. He knew if he were to go outside, the barefoot boy would run like a deer into the field of brush and weeds at the back of the church property. He made a decision to just watch him.

After a short time the boy walked to the front of the hall. All the time he kept his eyes to the ground. Twice he picked something up from the dirt and pocketed it. Father changed windows because the boy moved to the front of the church and continued to do the same thing. He was out of sight for awhile as he maneuvered back around the church to the rear. He stopped, held his head high to look both ways. He appeared to be checking to see if anyone was around. Not seeing anyone, he crossed the yard and entered the old shed where the Case tractor was kept.

Many times Father had caught sight of this boy on the property. Now was his chance to see what was going on. Carefully he slipped out the front door, and around the side of the house. He walked almost on tiptoe to not make noise. He made it to the back of the shed and down the side to get to the front door. Standing in the door he saw the boy with his back to him sitting on the old Case tractor. He watched the shirtless, tanned brown skinned, barefoot boy, as he sat on the tractor playing like he was the operator—turning the steering wheel, making motor sounding noises and make-believe shifting.

First Father cleared his throat, before he softly said, "I see you like my tractor."

A leap and the boy was on the ground in front of Father, who stood firm, blocking the exit.

Teeth locked tight, the boy spoke through them, "Better get out of my way." He reached into his pocket as if to draw something out and thrust that arm behind his back. "I've got a knife. I'll cut you."

"No you won't," Father said. "Besides, I'm not going to hurt you."

Jockeying for a position to run, the boy growled, "I'm tellin' you for the last time. Get out of my way. I mean...I am."

Shrugging off the remarks from the kid, Father relaxed his position and smiled as he said, "But I'm good. I want to be your friend."

A surprise came when the kid bolted right under his arm to escape. A short race and it was over. Father's legs being longer, he quickly ran beside the boy. The boy, knowing this, turned to his left to escape. Father dove to tackle him by grabbing his legs about the knees. Both were lying on the ground panting.

Before Father struggled to stand he held the boy by the waist. Upright, he was still holding the boy who kept fighting to get loose. His arms were flinging back and he kept kicking Father's legs.

After a few minutes the boy's strength began to diminish and he looked back at Father, and said, "I didn't steal nothing. I come to find the money on the ground. Let me go."

Father held him tight for a minute more. With his voice calm, he said, "You didn't steal. I saw you. The money was in the dirt. I trust you. I want to be your friend. You can walk around here anytime you wish without a worry. When the money is on the ground it's yours. What can I do to make you understand that?"

With his head turned back trying to see Father's face the boy said, "If you let me loose, I believe you, but you're not my friend."

Father released his grip about his waist, but held one of the boy's wrists. First the boy struggled, but soon gave that up, and asked, "Why you do this to me?"

"If I turn you loose, will you run? Promise you won't, and I'll let you go. We should talk."

It was obvious to the boy the man's strength was greater than his, and Father Bill was determined to detain him. Reluctantly, he said, "I do what you want if you let me go. Please."

Only a light hold was kept on the boy's wrist as Father again asked, "Your word...you promise?"

When the boy nodded, Father's arm dropped to his side. For another minute, it was a stand-off stare between the two. Father's stare was warm and the boy's was fear. It ended when Father extended his hand to shake, and said, "I'm Father Bill. You like sweetened tea? What's your name?"

The sun shone in his eyes as he squinted to see Father's face. With pride he said, "Tea...yes. I Stone Barberez. Honest. I do nothing wrong. Only found money on the ground."

"I know," Father said, and turned to go up to the house. "You go down there to one of those picnic tables and wait. I'll be right back with some tea for us."

Stone called to him, "You think I won't run?"

Father didn't look back, but spoke loud so Stone could hear him, "You'll not run. I know that for sure. You gave me your word."

They sat in the shade at a picnic table. Father enjoyed watching Stone watch the birds and naming each one that flew by. He also named butterflies and talked about grasshoppers, crickets, and spiders. Conversation was stilted until Stone looked directly at him and asked, "Do you like me?"

Father gave him his best smile. "Certainly I do. I think you're smart. You're strong, and I can trust you. We can be friends. Why do you ask?"

Stone looked down, swung his big toe back and forth in the dirt as he said, "My Dad says not to trust white man 'cause they don't like me. I think maybe no one likes me much as I'm half breed...half Indian and half Mexican. They don't like me either. I don't care. I can take care of myself."

Father wished to help and told him, "No one person is exactly like another. There have never been two exactly alike and there will never be. Everyone is an individual. Their own person. It makes no difference what race or color they are. Some people are good and others may only have some good about them. I think you may not have given them the opportunity to know you. You're a likeable guy. What about your mother? What does she think?"

He looked straight into Father's eyes. "I don't know. Maybe she like you." He placed his hand on his heart. "She's right here. With me all the time. Really good mother like your Mary Mother."

Father was not expecting that answer, but said, "Your Mother has passed over. I'm sorry. How long ago?"

Stone's face creased with happiness. "She greatest mother. When I was born I was little. Very little. Sick. Not strong. Goin' to die. She wanted me to live, so she give me her life. She took my place and died. My dad told me all about it. Many times he tells me. We both love her. A whole bunch."

Stone's story was very touching. Seeking more information from Stone, he asked, "What does your father do? Where do you live?"

The sun was back in Stone's eyes. He squinted as he pointed to the back side of the church property. "Down there 'aways'...cross the field and through the woods to the big ditch. Our little trailer at the big ditch. My dad, he work for farmer when he can get job. He good dad, but drink a lot. He did that after my mother died. I understand. He always good to me. Never hit me. We got each other."

Father still wished more answers. "You know about Mary, the Mother of Jesus. Where do you go to church?"

It was a bashful response when Stone said, "I do like when watch ball playin'. I sneak up to your window to listen. Back at the trailer I sing the same songs. Best, I like the prayer song, 'Our Father'. You do and say about the same all time. You have not learned another way? Bet I could almost do what you do."

Father explained, "Our Mass is always the same. It's the celebration of the Last Supper Jesus had with his disciples. You no longer have to sneak about. Come sit inside. If anyone asks, just tell them you're my friend."

Stone's face lit up as he asked, "You mean, maybe I could come after everyone is sat down. Be in back when it rains? No one sit back there durin' the week."

Father stood up. "Yes, anytime. I'd like to stay here a lot longer, but I've got to go to the barber shop for a haircut. I hope to see you often. Remember, we're now friends. You may come looking for coins about the hall and church anytime you wish." He extended his hand for a shake. "I'm looking forward to many good times—drinking tea with you, and you teaching me about nature."

As he walked up the hill toward his house, he watched Stone going home. He was no longer running as swift as the deer. Instead, his skipping steps were in rhythm to the musical sounds coming from him. Father stopped to listen. Yes, he was hearing, 'Gloria, Gloria, Hallelujah. Glory, Glory, Hallelujah. Glory, Glory, Hallelujah. His truth is marching on.'

Chapter 11

That evening as the trucks with the ballplayers arrived, Father walked down to find Ron to tell him about the offer for them to join a league in Javelle.

Ron was excited, and said, "Wait a minute." He turned around and whistled to get the other's attention. When the guys walked over, Ron said to Father, "Now tell that again." Everyone was thrilled and he barely finished as they talked about it with each other.

One voice above the others said, "We got a coach. Eddie Gable. He coached a boys' team when he lived in Poplar Bluff."

"Yeah. Eddie," everyone agreed.

Another voice sounded out, "We need a name and some shirts. How about St. Francis Bulls with red shirts?"

Father injected, "No. Not St. Francis. It would indicate you're all Catholic. You have the Men's Club. Maybe Quaintberg Men's Club...Bulls, Wolves, whatever. All you fellows are enjoying the hall which you brought back to life."

Wilber was serious when he asked, "Father, you had the idea. Are you sure you don't mind if it's not St. Francis something or other? I think you'd be a good coach."

"No, no," Father said, "I'm only here as the spiritual leader...not to be a coach, but thank you. My only request is that you make me proud by having the best darn ball team around." He wished to say, "And beat the pants off Father Morris' Sacred Heart Parish," but he knew that would be wrong.

The boys were listening and informed Father they wanted to form a team to join the league as well. The men were reluctant at first, but Father intervened for them.

As usual that evening Stone knelt at the edge of the meadow to watch the men play ball. Father motioned with his hand for him to come sit with him. After two tries, Father got off the bleachers and walked out to him. It was a short conversation. Soon Father's hand was on Stone's shoulder. They sat together and watched the game. At the end of the ninth inning, it was tied six to six. Stone knew he must leave before dark. He slipped off the bleacher, said goodnight to Father, and ran back to the meadow. It was in the tenth inning and almost dark, when Derek hit a homerun. Now there was the reason for the Men's Club to have fundraisers to buy shirts, hats, equipment and lights for the ball field.

Father's concentration was almost lost as he said Mass the next morning. In the back pew sat Stone. His hair was combed and he was wearing a nice shirt and pants. What Father couldn't see was that he was still barefoot.

The Mass ended. The last song selected was 'The Prayer of Saint Francis'. Father stepped off the altar into the aisle. Stone's second tenor, his perfect pitch voice rose above everyone's. When the others left, he walked back into the church to see Stone had moved up, right in front of the Blessed Virgin statue and was kneeling. Father was quiet as he backed out, and stood outside to wait for him.

Stone's eyes glistened when the door opened. He announced, "I feel good...like a man."

Father took him by the shoulder to lead him over to the house. "You are a man. Now I think it's time we had breakfast. Can you cook?"

Rose and Sis were already cleaning the house. Rose walked into the kitchen to find the two preparing to cook. "Hold on there. I just cleaned this kitchen. What do you two want to eat and I'll fix it. I'd rather cook than clean up your mess."

Sis was called to join them when the scrambled eggs, fried potatoes, sausage and biscuits were ready. Anything that might have been leftover was eaten by Stone.

After eating, Stone and Father went outside to sit at the picnic table again. Father asked when he might meet Stone's father.

"Dad should be back home by now," Stone told him. Earlier he went to Indian Joe's to feed the chickens, ducks, and check on him. They could go now.

"Wanna come with me?" Stone asked. "It's not far."

Father rose from the table. "Well, why not?"

Stone jumped to his feet to rush away.

Father called, "Hey, wait a minute! I'm older than you. Take it a little slow."

A blackberry bush scratched Father's left arm right after a wild rose bush brought blood on his right. Grass, weeds and scrub brush were above his waist. He was expecting a wide path but no—only a trampled area from Stone's feet. Father feared he might step on a snake as he followed the young man. He did pick up his pace, wanting to get through the area to the tall post oak trees and vines.

In the woods, the ground was covered with years of falling leaves, which made him less concerned about snakes.

Stone suddenly stopped and called back, "Wait. Be still. A blue racer snake is in front of me. You run, he'll chase you."

Father obeyed but wondered if he climbed a tree if the snake would follow. Next was an opening of green grass, and what he believed to be what Stone called the big ditch. Problem was the small, old trailer, Stone described, was on the other side. Stone dropped down over a foot, and the next time Father saw Stone's feet he was walking across the big ditch on the trunk of a tree that must have fallen more than a year ago. He stood there amazed at Stone's agility to walk on that thing. It looked like the longest log he'd ever imagined.

Stone called from the other side, "C'mon. You scared cat, no?"

Father called back, "Do I have to take off my shoes?"

Slightly annoyed at his friend, Stone called, "Oh, whatever."

Father sat down on the damp grass, removed his shoes and socks to hand-carry before he slid down to step on the fallen tree trunk. He thought he must look like a trapeze artist on a high wire, with arms outstretched, waving to balance himself. He was cautious as he placed one white bare foot in front of the other. All the time he kept asking God to please help him. Before he reached the other side, he promised God he would be a better priest if God would see him safely back to the rectory.

Pablo Barberez, Stone's father, was nothing like Father expected. Pablo was near Father's age, muscular built from years of laborious work and average height. After the greeting Pablo again sat down in one of the two, rickety, Adirondack chairs while offering the other to Father. Stone squatted in front of them to listen.

Father began, "Stone has been coming around the church and watching the ballgames. We're friends, so I wanted to meet you. He says you're having a bad time now because of so little work available this time of the year."

Pablo leaned forward, with an arm on the chair to look directly at Father. "You come thinking I'm not taking care of my son? You go right now."

Shaking his head, Father said, "Oh, no. You have me wrong. Stone says you're a very good father. I believe that. I was wondering if I might help you find work."

Pablo relaxed a little. "There will come hoeing and chopping in the field soon. Indian Joe lets us stay here now. Need help and old. I feed for him every day. Sometimes drive him into Sallow for supplies. Won't go to doctor like should. Gives some food and little money. I drink no more. If'n I do, Indian Joe say last time. Bye-bye. No drink for three weeks. Won't again. Do no good."

Father looked directly at him. "That's good. I've been told that's very difficult to do when you've been drinking for some time. I admire you for your strength."

Pablo sat back in his chair to say, "Drink off and on after Stone born. Lost his mother. My Buttercup. Young we were. She fifteen. Sixteen I. Her father Indian. See us talking—he beat her. Second time, I say to her, we leave or I kill him if he do it again. Stole horses from Indian Joe and left for Arkansas. Lot of farm work right then. My parents meet up with us. I start sending money to Indian Joe for horse. He, Stone's grandpa. Buttercup, she get sick when carry baby. We not move on with parents. Stone born. Little. Sick. I hold her and say, 'He so bony like rocks.' She laughed and said, 'We call him Stone'. Dad fall off ladder picking apples. Hurt back. They back in Mexico. If I gets big money, send 'em some."

Father broke in, "I believe you're a really good man who has had years of bad luck. How did you manage to work and take care of Stone?"

Field workers, we gots to lookout for each other. Not big enough to work in fields, kids watch little kids back at camp or under shade of tree. Schoolin' no. All time move. Stone, I want smart. Not work like us do. Indian Joe would take him, but Stone say no. I no like either."

Father's mind was working to find a solution. He remembered James Olheimer complaining about all the work at the Farmers' Market. In fact, a couple times, Olheimer had remarked about it growing so fast he needed help. "I just might know where you could get a job for the summer. A friend of mine runs a Farmer's Market on Highway PP. It's getting to be too much for him to keep the market going, and do the farming. Maybe you should talk with him."

Stone and Pablo were both excited and stood. Pablo asked, "Can you show me where to go? For no money, work for week to show I good. Take me?"

Father rose. "Well, I guess. They're almost always around the place. Your truck run?"

Pablo rushed to the trailer as he called, "You bet. Me wash a bit and comb hair. Change shirt. Be right back."

That was one bet Father should have taken. The truck only ran to a dry creek bed a couple miles away and died. Pablo left Stone and Father there in the shade, and took off running to borrow Indian Joe's truck.

While they waited, Stone picked up a handful of rocks and looked at Father. "See the bell on the wire. I ring it."

Five rocks and five times the bell rang. "Father asked, "Can you do that underhanded like a softball pitcher?"

"Yep." Stone selected five large rocks and rang the bell with each one.

Father was excited. "Can you do that with a ball?"

Stone had picked up another rock, and while ringing the bell stated, "No ball. No had one. Bet I could. "

Pablo returned with a better truck and Father directed him to Olheimer's Farm to make the introductions. Father and Stone exited by cutting through the field, leaving Pablo and Mr. Olheimer to talk.

Back at the rectory Father found a softball and two gloves. At the ball field, Father took the catcher's position, and sent Stone to the pitching mound. "Throw that ball right in my glove," Father said.

Many times Stone hit the mark before Father began to instruct him in ways to turn his wrist and how to properly hold the ball for the best control.

It wasn't long before the truck Pablo was driving came flying into the parking lot. The door flew open and Pablo, without even turning off the motor, came rushing to them. He picked up Stone, and whirled him around saying, "I gets it! I gets it! We sleep in barn and get food. Go gets our stuffs. Money good. One week. I be good. Make long time job. Come back tonight. Milk cows and feed."

Father reached to shake his hand. "Congratulations. Can Stone come to the ball game tonight? You can come, too."

Pablo had released Stone, but rubbed his head as he hugged him, "Sure. He come. Me got job. No come. Must go now. Come Stone."

Hand-in-hand they ran back to the truck.

Father was so excited he barely ate and kept checking the time on the clock over the refrigerator. Stone arrived but Father kept him in the house with him. That night the men were playing against the boys. Together they watched the trucks and cars arrive until it was almost time for the ball game to begin.

Father grabbed Stone's arm. "Okay. It's show time. Let's go," and he rushed him to the ball field and left Stone standing alone.

Father saw Wilber and called him to the side. He quickly told Wilber that his search for a pitcher might be over. Reluctantly, Wilber agreed to start Stone. Wilber motioned Stone over to give him the necessary instructions and walked away.

The men who were up to bat first were waiting. Wilber called David Stowe from the pitcher's mound to say he was to sit on the bench while he tried a new pitcher. It was Frank Talaman's turn to be the umpire that evening. Father took a seat on one of the bleachers.

Wilber patted Stone's back to say, "Go, boy, show me what you got."

Stone walked with pride to the mound, looked about to see all the players were in their proper position, wound up and pitched.

Frank called, "Strike one!"

The second pitch and Ron swung at the ball but missed. "Strike two."

Another pitch. Ron swung his best swing.

"Strike three."

Ron turned and looked toward Frank and asked, "How did I miss that one?"

Red Miller and then John Short also struck out.

The boys rushed in patting Stone on the back. The men slowly walked out to the field in shades of confusion and disappointment.

At the end of the first inning it was 1 to 0 in favor of the boys.

Eddie Gable, the men's coach, normally used the men's second string to play the boys, but changed plans. Derek was to take third base. He kept Ron, Red and John but replaced the others. After a talk, Derek was up to bat.

The first two pitches and Derek hit two foul balls but missed the third pitch.

"Strike three," called Frank.

Derek turned to Frank and said, "I don't see it that way. Are you sure that was a strike?"

"That was a great pitch," Frank said. It curved left just about your waist and right over the base. You swung too low."

Father was excited until it was Stone's turn to bat. He held the bat wrong and looked more like he was chopping wood. Father couldn't watch.

Strike three was called.

Father didn't realize Wilber had walked over to him to ask, "Now, you think you can teach that boy to bat? I could live with his chopping, but it's a little embarrassing. That kid's got a great arm."

"You?" Father asked, "How about me? I got so excited when I saw how he could pitch I forgot he would be up to bat. Think that may be the first time he ever held one. I'll start right after Mass tomorrow. I know he can do it."

The game ended with the boys, for the first time in a long time, beating the men. The score was 2 to 0.

There were many questions about the boy. Father called everyone over who was interested. With his hand on Stone's shoulder he began. "This young man is Stone Barberez. He and his father are new to the area. Stone is twelve years of age, but in the sixth grade. He has some catching up to do in that area. His batting practice will begin tomorrow morning. Stone, you did a fine job."

Applause broke out.

Stone could hardly wait to tell his father, and rushed across the field. Ron, Big Jane, and the Enstruckees remained to ask more questions about Stone's condition. Ruth volunteered to do tutoring plus take him to enroll in summer school. Big Jane and Ron invited Father to bring him to their house for clothes and shoes their son Josh had outgrown. Big Jane said she'd like to give him a regular haircut.

Soon Father learned the Olheimers moved Pablo and Stone from the barn into a spare bedroom in their house. Ruth's tutoring was exceptional. Stone did so well in summer school; they planned to start him in the eighth grade in the fall. His time with Father was trimming down since Mrs. Olheimer took a shine to him. She was helping to correct his English and began to teach him to play the organ. In return, Stone helped her with her housework and chores.

Every morning, Stone attended Mass. One fine morning, after Mass, they stood outside talking with Father. Mrs. Olheimer stated, "He hasn't replaced our son, who was killed in the war, but he's like another to me. In fact, sometimes I seem to think we've been blessed with two boys. Jim and Pablo get along so well. I don't know what we would have done had they not been sent to us."

Stone looked up to Father, and asked, "When can I go up and get the bread and wine? I'm ready, you know."

Father rubbed his head, "I taught you to pitch and bat, but that's not up to me. You must talk with your father and Mrs. Enstruckee."

The first time the Quaintberg Wolves played the boys from Father Morris' Sacred Heart Church, Father was certain his attitude was not pleasing God; however, he could hardly wait for the game to begin.

Stone easily struck out the first batter at Sacred Heart. Father looked toward Heaven and said, "I know this isn't right but I just can't help it. I'll get back with you tomorrow. Right now, I'm going to enjoy this game." Sitting with Ron, Big Jane, and the two Short families, his clapping and whistling was louder than anyone as he stomped his feet on the bleachers.

When the game ended the score was 4 to 0 favor the Quaintberg Wolves.

Father's throat was raw.

Chapter 12

The last Monday in August was the first day of school. When school was out in the afternoon, Father sat on his porch swing, and watched the school bus stop on Highway PP to let Stone and four other school children off who lived down Quaintberg Road. There was one boy almost a head taller than Stone, two girls about his size and two smaller boys. Their conversation was not audible, but when they were just past the general store, he saw the larger boy shove Stone backward. Stone shoved back only to be shoved again. They doubled up their fists and went at each other; however it stopped quickly as Stone knocked the bigger boy to the ground. He jumped on top of him and put his knees on the boy's arm muscles and slapped him across the face.

Father rushed over. He saw the bigger boy was crying. He bent down, wrapped one arm around Stone's stomach, and picked him up. He told the big boy, "Go ahead. Get up. You go first down the road."

When the boy was up, he ran with the three other kids following.

Father put Stone down, and said, "Well, you're a mess. Come with me, and I'll clean you up."

He found a few medicinal supplies to work on Stone's face. "What was that all about? You shouldn't be fighting."

Stone was still angry, and said, "He said you're a 'girly-man'. You wear dresses to church. I'm gonna make him take it back."

Father stepped back to look at him. "You were fighting for me? Buddy, let me fight my own battles. Don't you know you're not supposed to fight? God says you're to love your neighbor."

Stone snapped, "Love him! I don't even like him!"

"Maybe, if I knew him," Father said, attempting to explain, "I might not like him either, but we must love him. Not fight with him. Respect God's word."

Stone's response was to puff out air.

After he placed the supplies back into the cabinet, Father said, "I guess I'd better take you home, and explain to Mrs. Olheimer what happened. She'll be wondering where you are."

Stone smiled, "She'll be okay when I tell her today I got two A's. One in reading and one in math. She likes reading, and he likes math."

Returning from Olheimers, he noticed a deep blue BMW sitting in the church parking lot. It didn't happen too often; however, now and then someone might park there to meet someone, to check an address, etc. It was too far away from the rectory for him to be concerned. He went into the kitchen for a drink of water and sat at the table.

Through the kitchen window he watched a tall, very attractive lady with the most beautiful shoulder-length auburn hair he'd ever seen. She walked toward the rectory. The late afternoon sunlight played in her hair, flashing streaks of gold that matched the gold around her neck, her fingers and the bangles on her wrist. The fashionable, A-line, mint green dress was belted to accent her tiny waist.

As he walked toward his front door, he stopped to watch her through the picture window. He thought to himself, she has to be lost. No woman in Quaintberg ever dresses like that or drives a new BMW.

He opened the door before her long finger with the mother-of-pearl painted nail reached the doorbell.

"Hello, I'm Father Bill," he said. "Would you like to come in?"

Nervous tension was obvious as she hesitated a few seconds before replying, "Well, maybe it's all right. I'll just be a few minutes."

"Come on in," he said with what he believed to be his best smile. "No rush. I have nothing planned. Stay as long as you like." Then a thought came to him, and he questioned himself, Bill, are you acting like a priest, or like the ol' Bill before you went into the seminary? Get a hold on yourself. She's drop-dead gorgeous, but *you're* a priest!

Clutching her purse, she stepped just far enough in to allow the storm door to close, and stated, "I came to see what happened to the basket for the donations for the hall."

He motioned toward the nearest chair, and said, "Have a seat. We're so fortunate. The hall is complete plus the church redecorated. It's all paid in full. We owe nothing. That was a surprise to me and many...both are really paid."

She sat with a professional demeanor on the edge of the chair. "That's almost impossible. I'm a business woman, so I have some idea of the costs. Are you certain, or was it for some other reason it was removed?"

Sitting across from her on the couch, he reported, "It's true. Every penny of it was paid and with a small amount left over. How is it you have an interest? I remember noticing you a couple of times sitting in the back of the church, but don't recall you participating in any of the activities."

She smiled, but a little sarcasm rang in her voice when she said, "I see you don't know who I am, but you must have heard stories. Some true, and I suspect most were not."

After an attempt to recall, he uttered, "I don't know your name. Maybe I have, but I seldom listen to gossip."

She relaxed, and said, "I believe you. I'm Marg O'Money Wright. My late husband, Lawrence Wright, was born and raised here. He, like his father, Eugene Wright, was an architect. His father's first project was to design and build your hall. I'm so thankful it's been restored. The roof is exactly like the one on Wright Farm's big barn."

"That's interesting." Father leaned forward. "It is unusual. Where do you live?"

"I'm from Newark, New Jersey. I have a home there, and an apartment in New York. Lawrence brought me here twice. When he died, I inherited forty-percent interest in the Wright Farm, but Hawk manages it well. I trust him.

"When my husband fell from the balcony on the second floor, I was immediately arrested for his death. Witnesses told the law officials, we fought all the time, and they heard us fighting just before he fell. Of course, it wasn't true, and I was acquitted. It was possibly the biggest trial this county ever had. Many couldn't get into the courtroom, and had to stand outside. I left immediately when it was over. That was about five years ago. When Hawk told me the hall was to be rehabbed, I knew Lawrence would want me to return and make a donation to see its completion. I'll mail you a check soon. You may use it where you wish since the hall is complete. I'm going home. To tell you the truth, I'm not at all comfortable at the farm. There's too much going on there. According to Hawk, it's been that way for years and years."

Father stood. "Have you seen the inside of the hall? If not, I'd be glad to show it to you."

She slipped past him to the porch, and said, "Thank you, but I don't think you should. I've probably stayed in here with you too long already. People around here love to talk. I must be going." With her back to him, she called, "Thanks. Have a good evening."

He stood with the door open to watch her rush to her car. She backed up and headed out without a wave or honk.

The same evening Big Jane, Little Jane, Kate Freehill and Peggy Short dropped by to discuss plans for a card party. After Father was briefed, a date was set.

He believed it might be a good time to learn more about his previous visitor, and asked, "You all must have known Lawrence Wright and his wife, Marg. Tell me about them."

The four women looked at each other before Big Jane began, "Well, where do we start? That place would make a good book, except no one would believe it was true."

Kate, lightly teasing, said, "Don't tell me she came to see you? Father, she's not Catholic. Better be careful."

"Honey, none of 'em are Catholic," Big Jane said. "Maybe...except for some of those Mexicans. I've been seeing a fancy BMW fly by now and then. So she's back. I'd better keep an eye on good ol' Ron. He goes for them red-headed women. Lot's wrong with him but not his eyesight."

More curious than ever, Father asked, "What all goes on there?"

"All I know is what I've heard," Little Jane said. "It goes all the way back to when Lawrence's father bought over a thousand acres and began to build. He was an architect and traveled a lot. Understand he always had a girl at every job. Even here, he was thick with that Indian gal until he got her pregnant. At the same time, his wife was pregnant with Lawrence."

Peggy noted, "Got to give 'im credit. He took care of them...the Indians...financially. Heard he first moved her to Colorado with her son, Hawk. Even put him through college. Now he's manager and part owner of Wright Farm."

"Yeah, nice guy," Big Jane said. "When his wife started raising hell about his excursions, she choked to death on something. The coroner told my dad it was the first time he ever saw bruises on anyone's neck from choking on a piece of beef. Of course, ol' Doc Dowell's dad would swear to anything for money."

Little Jane laughed, "The Dowells all fall from the same tree. All alike if you ask me. Guess justice was when ol' Earnest Wright himself fell into his own lake and drowned after Lawrence married that Bee gal. Bee, Beatrice, Jean or whatever she called herself. Everyone knew he was a good swimmer. So why did he drown?"

Peggy added, "Funny, Earl Sneakel happened upon him. Ten o'clock at night and he just happened to take a walk down to the lake. Said he got wet 'cause he jumped in trying to save ol" Earnest."

Father was laughing when he said, "The way you're telling it, there were a lot of misfortunes. This Bee...where is she now?"

Big Jane emitted a bark of laughter, and said, "Dead, too!! Course she was a character. Liked them good-looking Mexican men. One...that Juan, got her pregnant. She was going to get an abortion, but when Juan heard about it, he threatened to go to the law about the illegals' working there. She went out of state until the baby girl was born. Then she gave it to Juan and his wife, Rosetta."

Kate asked, "Didn't Bee lose the first baby? Lawrence's baby?"

93

"Ha, according to Doc Dowell there never was a baby," Big Jane said. "She just claimed it to get Lawrence to marry her. He'd never done it otherwise. Those Sneakels are nothin' but white trash."

"They did pretty good," Peggy said, "She and that brother, Earl, living like royalty in the compound at Wright Farm."

Trying to keep it straight in his mind, Father asked, "Where does Marg fit into the picture?

"After the baby girl affair," Peggy began, "they called her Juanita. Lawrence wanted a divorce. Bee kept fighting it. He finally gave up, and just brought that gal, Marg O'Money, from up East to live with him in another wing of the house. After they moved in, Bee overdosed on drugs and alcohol. Only a week after she was on the root side of the grass, they flew back East and got married. Maybe they stayed up East for a year before they returned. They weren't back here more than a couple weeks, when early one morning he walked out on the balcony on the second floor and fell off. Killed him!"

Little Jane laughed, "Ain't anyone believed that except for that six man jury."

"Ain't a man in the world would vote to hang a body like hers," Big Jane said, "or that skinny little blond lawyer she brought with her. When I go to Heaven I want a body just like that. People will stop saying, Jane, you have such a pretty face. It's a cover up 'cause I know I have an ugly body."

Peggy wasn't finished with the story. "Father, I think the best one yet is that Earl Sneakel, Bee's brother. After Bee died, he went to court to prove the little girl, Juanita, was Bee's daughter, and became her guardian. Granted guardianship, he fought for her percent of the estate. The court granted her twenty-percent. Tom and John have both worked on the electricity down there and say Rosetta and Juan still have the girl living with them."

Little Jane turned to Father, "Why did she come to see you?"

"She wanted to know about the finances for the hall," he replied. "I told her it's paid in full. That was it."

"That's it! Kate said. "The gold dollars in the basket. No one around here has gold dollars."

"You're right," Peggy said. "It must have been her. Lawrence's father built the hall."

"She's got big bucks," Big Jane said. "I'm going to tell her Lawrence built my house. Maybe she'll give me some of them gold dollars."

The next morning after Mass, Father walked back into the church to see the short, stocky, middle-aged, Mexican woman still kneeling in prayer, so he continued down the aisle to extinguish the candles.

"Father, good," she said. "Confess please."

He continued to walk up and around the pews to the confessional. In a moment he heard her kneel on the other side.

She began, "Padre above. Forgive me my sins. 'Special my worsts. My girl to keep, I lied. I no ever hear 'em fight. They love only. Understand no? It hurt Mrs. Wright. Good lady. Do wrong I, but maybe someday I fix. Long time no Mass or confess. Know it really bad. Padre, please forgive." She began to cry and speak only in Spanish for a short time.

Father didn't know any Spanish, but when she stopped, he suggested she go kneel and pray until she felt better.

In his mind, parts of the puzzle were still missing, but he chose not to dwell on it.

Back in the rectory, he poured himself a second cup of coffee and sat down to read the *St. Louis Review* when the doorbell rang.

It was Marg again and very upset. "Is Rosetta with you?" she asked. "She was to wait for me on Highway PP. Juan dropped her off, and I was to pick her up."

Father replied, "No. The Mexican woman? No—she's not here. She left the church about ten minutes ago—headed that way."

"Sorry to have disturbed you," Marg said. "I'm so worried. I've driven up and down the road a few times. Can't imagine where she went."

"She's probably all right," Father replied. "Some folks know their way through the fields and woods. I think she may be home soon."

He forgot all about the Wright Farm that afternoon, and worked on his new jigsaw puzzle.

Around dark, a county sheriff's car pulled into his drive. A sharply dressed young man got out and started toward the house. Father opened the door to meet him and asked, "How can I help you?"

The broad shouldered, stocky, athletic-built young deputy said, "I'm Deputy Duck. A woman's been reported missing. Are you Father Bill?"

"Yes."

"She's a Mexican woman. Middle aged. Typical Mexican, I guess. Does have legal papers. I was told you may have been the last to have seen her. What's your story?"

Father was surprised, and said, "I hope nothing's wrong. She came to Mass this morning. When Marg O'Money-Wright came looking for her, I told her, the last I saw of her, she was walking toward PP. I don't know anymore."

Deputy Duck took a step back. "Well, okay, Father. Just doing my duty. Not too concerned. Those Mexicans are always going and coming...legals and illegals. Don't give us many problems. You have a good evening."

A good evening it was not for Father. Rosetta was on his mind. He said aloud, "How could she be missing? It doesn't make sense."

He slapped his hand on his head, and said, "Boy, you are doing it again. Talking to yourself out loud. Maybe you need something to talk to around here...a bird or something. At times it does get lonesome."

He stood. "May as well go to bed. I'll need to say many prayers to get to sleep tonight."

He stopped to reflect. "Gee, I don't think I said that out loud. Good. I really don't want a bird."

Chapter 13

Father, though his head just hit the pillow had fallen into deep sleep for only a few minutes, when someone rang his doorbell again and again.

He sat up in bed, turned, and swung his legs over the edge. He rubbed his face and ran his fingers through his hair before slipping into his pants. As he stood, he said to himself, this day has been about enough to make a priest cuss.

Barefoot, he ambled into the living room, and opened the door to face two men. One was wearing a ski mask and the other a bandana over his face. He growled, "Fellers, if this is trick or treat you've come to the wrong house."

The man in the front raised a pistol, and pointed it at him. "Open this damn storm-door, Priest-man. Now we're gonna hear your confession."

"Open it yourself," Father snapped. "It's not locked," and he stepped back.

The two walked in. The man in front still held the pistol pointed at Father, and demanded, "Okay, tell us all you know about Rosetta. We know she talked with you. If you lie, I'll give you a ticket to hell with this right now," and he shook the gun for emphasis.

"Last I saw her she was walking toward Highway PP," Father said. "I have no idea where she went from there."

The man in the back said with a raspy voice, "No. We wanna know what she told you. You'd better start talking. He's got an itchy finger."

The man with the pistol took a step closer to Father. He was in range now. Father slightly turned, and with his right arm gave the man a backhand chop to his throat. Accidentally, the man pulled the trigger causing a bullet to whiz past Father's arm and lodge into the wall. Father gave him an upper cut just below the breast bone with his left hand, and the man dropped the gun. Then he followed up with a kick to the groin.

The man doubled up on the floor. The other man made a dive for the gun. He caught Father's hard chop to the back of his neck, spilling him over his partner.

Father picked up the gun, and sat on the couch. Both were either unconscious or afraid to move and lay still for some time. He knew in time they would stir.

Father could see fear in the eyes of the man on top as he rose to his knees. His voice was firm when he ordered, "Get your buddy up and get out of here. Now! It's late."

The other man moved and sat up. He slurred, "Damn, I got a headache."

He was close enough for Father to give him a hard kick to his thigh as he said, "Let me give you fellows some advice while you're still alive. Don't wake a hibernating bear and don't tick me off. You got one minute to get out of here before I call the law."

As they rushed out, he called, "Don't you dare come back here for the pistol. I'm keeping it."

The next morning he rose, made his bed and coffee while waiting for seven o'clock. He was pretty sure that was when when Deputy Duck came on duty.

The phone only rang once before Deputy Duck answered.

"Hi," Father began, "Remember me from St. Francis in Quaintberg? Father Bill. Last night I had a couple of uninvited guests asking about that missing Mexican woman. Messed up my living area. Put a bullet hole in the wall."

Deputy Duck's anxious voice asked, "Are you all right? Where are they?"

Father assured him he was fine, and that they were gone. He continued to tell him the whole story which excited the deputy.

Deputy Duck cut in, "Hold on, Father. I'll be right out there. You should have called last night when they left. Actually you should have held them until one of the night shift deputies could get there to arrest them."

Shaking his head, Father said, "I'm not the law. Don't know if I could have held them. No sense having the law rush out here with lights and siren. That would have woken everyone up in Quaintberg. You say you're coming out? Do me a favor. Bring me a couple apple-fritters from Hilga's Bakery. Haven't had one of those for awhile."

Sitting at the table with a cup of coffee and an apple-fritter, Deputy Duck asked, "Where did you learn to fight like that? Weren't you scared?"

Father gave a confident smile when he said, "You wouldn't know about it, but I was born and raised in Dogtown in South St. Louis. I'm Irish. Other babies cry when they're born. Irish babies scream. The three characteristics of the Irish are, they like to eat, drink and fight. Dogtown is right across the highway from the Italians living on the Hill. They're fighters, too. It was a war with us kids. The finest bakery in St. Louis is The St. Louis Bakery, an Italian bakery on the Hill. They're big, but never had signs painted on their delivery trucks for fear we would rock them when they drove through Dogtown to make deliveries."

Deputy Duck took the last swig of his coffee, and stood. "I think I'll take a ride over to Wright Farm. Would you like to come with me?"

Carrying the cups to the sink, Father replied, "If you don't mind. I'd like to see that place."

Deputy Duck turned off Highway PP to the right onto a narrow, gravel road overgrown with grass. It made a ninety degree turn to the right and continued on for a about a quarter of a mile before it turned left again. The compound was well-hidden by trees and brush from the highway. A quarter of a mile more and there was a guard-house at the gate. On the opposite side of the gate everything was beautifully manicured. Deputy Duck rolled down the car window to speak to the guard. "We're here to see Hawk Wright, the manager."

The poker-faced Mexican guard said, "No message he see you. Sorry. Private property."

Deputy Duck pulled out his badge and stated, "I'm with the sheriff's department. Call him."

Father and Deputy Duck made small talk about the large size of the compound while they waited.

From the guard-house the guard went directly to open the gate. When the Deputy's car was even with the guard, he instructed, "Go direct to end. Left turn. Follow road. Mr. Wright townhouse last at end. No. 7 on stone by door."

A maid answered when Deputy Duck rang the bell, but Hawk called, "Mariana show the gentlemen into my office. I'll be right with them."

The Deputy and Father were seated only a minute before Hawk and a woman entered. He was mysteriously handsome— tall, trim, with deep olive skin and distinguished gray sideburns. His deep brown eyes could pierce your soul. He turned to the woman, he'd introduced as his administrative assistant, "Dori take a break. Be back in fifteen minutes."

He nodded to Deputy Duck as he said, "Hello, nice to see you again." To Father he extended his hand, "Lawrence Eugene Wright, Jr., everyone calls me Hawk, my Indian name. I prefer that."

Father stood. "Bill. Father Bill. I'm the priest at St. Francis."

Hawk motioned for Father to sit. "Pleased to meet you. Marg told me about you."

No one heard her coming, but Marg appeared in the door barefoot, wearing a bathrobe and her hair covered in a towel twist. The surprise on Father's face was obvious. She gave him a friendly smile showing all those pretty, straight white teeth, and said, "Father, I'm not comfortable living in mine and Larry's quarters, so I'm staying with Hawk. His guest. We knew each other in college." She laughed, "He was my husband back then for almost forty eight hours. We ran away and got married. When my father heard about it, he found us, and had the marriage annulled. I was sent to Europe for three years. It was a surprise to both of us when Larry brought me here. We'd not seen or heard from each other after the day of the annulment."

Hawk smiled with admiration when he asked Marg, "Honey, why don't you join us? You might like to hear what these gentlemen have to say."

She slipped into a nearby chair and carefully pulled the bottom of the robe to show less of her long, shapely legs.

Her eyes reflected happiness when she looked at Father to say, "So nice to see you again, Father. If you ride, maybe someday Hawk and I could show you around the property."

Father was pleased, but reported, "Thanks, but I'm a city boy. I've never been on a horse—afraid of cows, pigs, and even little dogs."

Deputy Duck wanted to get to business and interrupted, "The reason Father and I are here is that he had two unwanted visitors last night. They came seeking information about Rosetta. Did a little damage to his house."

Marg was most interested, "Who were they?" She turned to Father, "Hope they didn't hurt you."

Shaking his head, Deputy Duck blurted, "No. Father wasn't hurt. He allowed them to go after one took a shot at him. They had covered their faces. One appeared to be a bit older than the other. About normal size men. One wore jeans, and the older guy was wearing dark blue pants. They wanted to know what Rosetta said to him. He believes he would recognize the eyes and voices if he were to see them again. Do you have any records of who left or returned to the compound last evening?"

"I'll call the guard shack for them to bring the register," Hawk said. "In fact, I'll go meet the guard."

He excused himself to go to another room to make the call.

Marg stood and called, "Hawk, I'll take Father out to see the St. Francis Grotto while we wait." She turned back to Father. "It's beautiful. Larry loved it so much."

They followed her out. She gave them an account of her deceased husband's daily activities. "Our bedroom was on the second floor at the end of the other wing. Exactly at six-thirty every morning the maid brought coffee and some sweets. It was Larry's request, or I should say orders. He did everything by the clock. By that time he would have been out of the bathroom and dressed. After he drank his first cup of coffee, he would go out on the balcony to lean out to see around the wall. He was happy if the bird-feeders were full. He insisted the birdbaths be cleaned and filled with fresh water each morning before he rose. When he came back in, he would tell me which flowers were in bloom that day. He was a nature man. He loved trees, shrubs, flowers and all the little creatures on the farm. Hawk often teased him saying, 'If it was left up to Larry, Wright Farm would grow nothing but flowers, trees, and shrubs."

They stood for a few minutes to admire the craftsmanship of the large, beautiful, life size St. Francis statue, hand-sculptured from Italian marble. It was surrounded by an abundance of a variety of blooming flowers. Shrubs and evergreens were in the background before the tall, semicircle, cascading waterfalls.

"Think we better be getting back," Deputy Duck said. "I have lots on my agenda for today."

When they turned around the corner of the building, Father stopped to watch a man talking with Hawk. He interrupted Marg to say, "Stop, please. That guy looks familiar. Yes, I believe he may be the older guy. Who is he?"

"Him? Marg asked, "that's Earl Sneakel."

"Quiet," Father ordered. "I want to see if I can listen to that voice."

The three barely breathed.

After a minute Father turned to Deputy Duck to quietly say, "I'd like to see his eyes. His size and voice is very near to the older one last evening."

"Earl," Deputy Duck called out, "over here. We want to talk with you."

Earl turned toward them. Seeing Father and the Deputy, he made a run for his truck, but realized he wasn't going to make it. In desperation, he turned to run up the hill toward the woods. Hawk and Marg were stunned and stood silent. Father and the deputy were in pursuit. Father's legs were longer, and he was the fastest.

For a few seconds he ran beside Earl, then like a football player he made the tackle. Earl went down face first, sliding several inches on the damp grass. Father was right was on top and straddled him.

Deputy Duck caught up, but stood as a spectator. Hawk, Marg and several others ran to watch.

Father grabbed Earl's arm and pulled it up behind him.

"Let me go! Earl demanded, "you're about to break my arm. I want a lawyer."

Father pulled harder on his arm, and said, "I'm a priest. I'm ready to hear your confession. Where's Rosetta?"

Earl moaned as he said, "I don't know. Damn it let me up! I have my rights."

"Ow," he screamed again. "Please! You're gonna break my arm."

Father gave it another yank. "You'd better talk or I'll break both your arms before I do your legs and your head. Where is Rosetta?" He grabbed the other arm and pulled it back.

"Damn you!" Earl cried. "She's down at the slaughter house. She's okay. Let me up."

"That'a boy. All right. Who came with you to visit me last night?"

When Earl hesitated, Father gave another yank.

"Ow!" Earl screamed, "Jed, my cousin."

Father smiled, "You're doing good now. Keep it up. You're going to feel better. Now talk to me about the railing on the balcony. What part did you play in Lawrence's death?"

Earl stammered, "You damn ba..."

Like lightning Father's hand swooped down over Earl's mouth almost cutting of his air. He bent over to Earl's right ear, but was audible when he whispered, "Watch your mouth. Remember this is your confession time and there are ladies present. I don't like that kind of talk." Sitting up straight again he yanked both Earl's arms up toward his head.

Earl withered with pain and cried, "I didn't do it! Honest. I can't stand it anymore. Rosetta is okay. Send someone to see for yourself."

Father shoved on both arms again, and his voice was serious when he said, "This is your last chance. I'm getting tired. If you don't want them broken, talk to me about the railing. Talk and talk fast."

"Oh, God!" Earl screamed, "Juan loosened the railing! He did it. Please. Let me up."

Father leaned down to Earl's ear again and said, "Just between us boys. Why did he do it?"

Earl was almost breathless when he replied, "He thought Lawrence was going to send him away again."

Juan was in the crowd and immediately stepped forward. He stammered, "I did do it. I did, but not for same reason. Earl said he would get rid of Juanita if I no do it. That would kill my Rosetta. I prayed the fall no kill him. I no want my Rosetta or my Juanita girl hurts."

"Juan," Deputy Duck ordered, "stay right here. Wait a minute. I trust you. Take someone with you and go get Rosetta."

Father bopped up and down on Earl's back. "Come on, boy. You're gonna feel better when it's all out. You'll no longer live in fear." He shoved Earl's arms up toward his head again. "Why did you drown Lawrence's father?"

"How did you know? Jesus, that was a long time ago," Earl muttered.

Riding his back like a horse, Father said, "True, but this is now. Better tell me the truth."

Earl was weak, but able to utter, "He was never going to allow me on Wright Farm again. He and I were both after the same woman. I was the better man. He would've drowned me."

Father let go of his arms and stood. He brushed the dirt off his hands as he looked at Deputy Duck. "Sheriff, he's all yours. Guess you heard all of it and have witnesses as well."

Deputy Duck reached down and handcuffed Earl. "Hawk, would you have a couple men carry him down to my car and put him in the back seat?"

Father and Deputy Duck fell behind the crowd as they walked back down the hill. Deputy Duck said, "You saved the department a lot of time and the county a lot of money. You don't know how many times I wanted to do just what you did, but that would be illegal for me."

Father was curious and asked, "It's not for me, is it?"

Deputy Duck broke into loud laughter. "Reckon not. Aren't priests supposed to listen to confessions? Bring out the best in people. That one was a dandy." He slapped Father on the back. "Damn, Father, you're sure good at your job. Wait a minute. I didn't hear you give him any 'Hail Mary's' or 'Our Father's! Nothing for penance?"

Father was laughing too, and said, "Leave it to the judge."

Chapter 14

Riding back to the Rectory, Deputy Duck turned on the radio to hear, "Breaking news. The missing Mexican woman from Wright Farm has been found unharmed. She had been kept tied in one of the Wright Farm buildings. Details are not clear; however, we are led to believe the priest from St. Francis of Assisi forced a confession from the guilty party. We have a reporter on the way to Wright Farm and will keep you updated".

Deputy Duck turned off the radio. "Father, it'll be no time until they come to get your story. My advice is that you prepare ahead of time what you wish to say. I must warn you that whatever you say will not be printed word for word. No. They're drama writers knowing their readers like sensationalism. I'll be radioing ahead for a couple of men from the sheriff's department to come out to control traffic at the rectory and Wright Farm. We can't keep them off the church property—it's public, but we'll be able to keep them off your yard and driveway."

"What will I tell them?" Father asked. "I don't want to be a part of it. I'm just a priest out here."

Deputy Duck laughed, "Afraid it's a little too late now. You're going to have a short time of fame...radio and newspapers. This is a big story for them. In no time they'll be here, possibly from as far away as St. Louis and Springfield. Right now it appears they may only know about the Mexican woman. Wait till they find the joker in the back seat was involved in Lawrence Wright's death. That's big."

Wishing for advice, Father asked, "Should I leave? Go some place? How soon will they leave? I don't want to talk with reporters. "

Deputy Duck was trying hard to control his laughter since he liked Father. "Father, you should have thought about that before you took on those two last night. Even kept their pistol. Remind me, I have to take that to the station. Then you tackled Earl—forced a confession. You made him confess to everything—even Lawrence Wright's father's drowning years ago. Man, you're big news. I'm sorry, but every radio station and newspaper will want to hear your story."

With disgust Father said, "I may not talk. I don't like publicity. They'll have to understand, I'm just a small country priest that was caught up in that mess."

Deputy Duck stopped in the rectory drive to let him out. "So you say, but that's not the way they're going to see it. Not many men could or would have done what you did. You're my hero. Someday, I'll be telling my grandkids about this day. Try to relax and enjoy the rest of the day. We'll do our best to keep the press away. When this blows over, I'd like to buy you dinner."

Father hardly had time to wash-up and change his grass stained jeans before Rose and Big Jane arrived to see if he was all right. Rob Blue came from across the street as well as Mr. Gruder. Rose made a pot of coffee, and they sat around the kitchen table to hear his watered-down story. Big Jane fielded the telephone calls for Father because he didn't wish to talk with anyone.

Going to pour another cup of coffee he noted, "The biggest thing for me to face now is going to be the reporters. I don't want to talk with them, but Deputy Duck is sure they'll be coming."

Mr. Gruder piped up, "So's all right. I jest go outside and tell 'em they's not welcome. Reckon they'd better git goin'."

Rose said, "No you can't do that. It might make some matters worse."

"I could handle it," Big Jane spoke. "Father, if you don't want to talk with them, write something for me to report as your assistant."

The doorbell rang, and Big Jane went to answer it. "Yes?"

The man outside stated, "I'm Jess Dotell with Radio Station KCKN. I want to talk with the priest."

In her most professional voice she replied, "Sorry. He's not able to see anyone. I'll have a statement for the press from him at eleven o'clock. You may come back then."

The reporter had stepped to a position not allowing the storm door to shut. He leaned to look in and asked, "Is he all right? I understand he had a fight with one of the men at Wright Farm. Last evening, according to one source, someone shot him. Were you with him or what has he told you? Is he here now?"

She tried to smile, and said, "Physically, he's fine but tired. He's resting."

"And you are?" The reported asked.

"His assistant." She smiled.

The reported asked, "And your name?"

"I have nothing more to say."

The photographer with the reporter raised his camera, and asked, "Do you want me to take any pictures?"

Big Jane, being one of little patience, looked directly at him, and said, "You click that thing at me and I'll make you eat it! Now get out of here!" and slammed the door.

Rob and Mr. Gruder left, but Rose and Big Jane remained.

Father wrote and rewrote five times before handing the statement to Big Jane to read. She read aloud, "Last evening two men came here asking about Rosetta, the missing Mexican woman. I offered no information to them except that she left the church building and walked toward Highway PP. This morning a sheriff's deputy came by and asked me to ride with him to Wright Farm. While we were there a man resembling one of the men who came calling last evening was spotted. I reported it to the deputy. The deputy arrested him and brought me back to the rectory."

She looked at Father and asked, "That's it. You said he confessed to you? I hope you beat the crap out of him! I don't know if they're going to believe this."

Soft-spoken Rose said, "Now, Jane, Priests don't physically attack people. Father is a kind man. I think Father's statement's good."

Big Jane threw her hands up, "All right, if that's what you all want. Me? I like blood and guts. Wish I'd been there. I'd like to slap him around, myself, for that poor woman...then kick his butt for all the other things he did."

Two deputies arrived to keep the reporters away from the house.

While they waited for eleven o'clock, Big Jane turned on the radio to hear, "Earl and Jed Sneakel were arrested today at Wright Farm for the kidnapping of Rosetta Gomez, the housekeeper at Wright Farm. Last evening they went to the rectory at St. Francis of Assisi in Quaintberg. For a time they held Father McHeck at gunpoint. This morning, a deputy took Father McHeck to Wright Farm for a look around. When Father McHeck recognized Earl Sneakel as one of the men who held him hostage last night, Earl started to run. Father McHeck grabbed him as Earl fought to get loose.

"There were several by-standers, but no one volunteered to stop the fight or help the priest. During the fight, McHeck forced Earl to confess he and Jed Snealel kidnapped the Mexican woman. The fight continued for some time until a deputy handcuff him. We understand, since his arrest, Earl has also confessed to paying a laborer to loosen the railing at Wright Farm causing Lawrence Wright to fall to his death. The sheriff's office reports Earl is not physically hurt except for several bruises, a sprained arm, and a couple of small cuts.

"The whereabouts of Father McHeck and his condition remain unclear. On the phone, we were told he is unable at this time to talk with the press. From the condition of Earl, it's doubtful the priest is in much better shape—possibly worse.

"There have been conflicting reports as one source said one of the men shot Father McHeck in the arm last evening. Another said Father McHeck beat-up both men causing them to leave. The parishioners at St. Francis have aided Father McHeck to avoid interviews before. For the time being he still remains our mystery priest. Stay tuned, and we will continue to report the story as it unfolds."

Promptly at eleven two deputies led Big Jane to the front steps of the church. She read Father's statement and took no questions. Disappointment was clear, but slowly the cars with reporters and photographers moved away, except for two.

At eleven thirty Rob Blue brought lunch to the three and stayed awhile to chat. About twelve-thirty everyone prepared to leave. Big Jane carried a key and pretended to lock the door as if the house was empty. The two remaining reporters followed Big Jane's car as she drove away.

Father was left alone to wrestle with his actions from the past night and morning. He realized priests are not supposed to be violent; however he couldn't think of another way he could have acted.

He realized earlier that Rob had disconnected his phone to avoid calls, so he plugged it back in for service.

Three minutes later it rang, and he answered.

The voice on the other end said, "Bill, this is Archbishop Cannon. We've been trying to reach you for a long time. Where have you been?"

Father replied, "Here, but had the phone disconnected for awhile. Some things are happening around here, and I didn't want to talk with anyone."

Archbishop Cannon's voice rose as he said, "Some things happening! You're all right, aren't you? It's on the radio stations here in St. Louis. Since we couldn't reach you, Bishop Gunn called the sheriff's office and received a report from a Deputy Duck. I assume it's correct. Lad, you have us all concerned about your safety. Twice I talked with your grandmother to tell her I believed you must be fine. You'd better call the family.

"Now what's this about you being in a fight? You were a rough kids, but you're a priest now and priest's don't fight. Always had my doubts about you, but your grandmother kept telling me you would change for the better...give you time. Deputy Duck said you threatened to break a man's arms. We assigned you down there where it would be quiet to test your abilities. You keep breaking the rules like restoring a church which was to be closed. That hall. I know you had an addition built onto it without permission. Don't know where you got the money for anything. We had to learn about all of it from the insurance adjustor. Yet, you keep claiming you don't need a loan for anything."

Bill was smiling. "That's true, Archbishop, but I didn't do anything...the parishioners did all of it. I'm inviting you down here some Sunday to say Mass and meet them."

The Archbishop's voice was matter-of-fact. "Bill, to tell you the truth, I don't know if I should leave you there. It could be you'd be better to serve if I brought you back up here to St. Louis to work on administrative duty. I've been thinking that for some time. I guess I would have already done it; however, Bishop Gunn and your grandmother, too, keep saying I should give you more time. They think what you're doing is good and you'll mature. You know your grandmother and I have been good friends for many years. I'd hate to disappoint her."

Father Bill was slightly annoyed and said, "Archbishop Cannon, let me ask you—if someone took a shot at you, would you just turn the other cheek? If that's true, then maybe you should be the Pope. I can't do that. When I see wrong, I want to make it right. When I see bad I want to make it good. When a person has a gift I would like to see him use it. Tell me, is that wrong? You can remove me, but the parishioners here are the best. The church is growing and so is the community. You should give them credit."

The Archbishop's voice was now cheerful when he said, "Hold on there, Bill, you're sounding like Rebecca McHeck. You got a lot of her in you. I respect that Irish gal. When she doesn't agree with me, she stands right in my face to tell me. Always has. For now, Bill, I'll leave things stand as is, and see what happens from here. Don't get into another fight! Bishop Gunn is already working with the press here to quiet things down. This isn't good publicity for us. Refer all questions to us. And don't be building down there without permission—whether they have the money or not."

Father Bill's 'tick' was gone and he responded, "Archbishop, I think you for calling and your concerns. I love my job. I love my flock. I do wish you would come one time and say Mass on Sunday. The parishioners would love to have you. Did you know both the men and boy's baseball teams won first place in their divisions? I know you'd enjoy watching them play. They're really good."

The Archbishop laughed, "And I guess you had nothing to do with that, either?"

Father's voice was light when he said, "No sir, I'd like to play again, but I know the rules. You know I was darn good on first base. My contribution is only to cheer for my team."

The Archbishop was still laughing and teased, "You bet, Bill. It just so happened that nine adults and nine teenagers, on their own, decided to organize two teams and beat the pants of every other team in their leagues. I understand, you now have a lighted baseball field down there on church property. And while I'm talking with you...what's this about you requesting a contest regarding religion between your teens and Father Morris's teens? He says you're always bragging that your teens are better educated and smarter than his. Bill, you should be saving souls, not beating others in competition."

Father's final words were, "You're right, sir. I'll remember that."

That night after he said his prayers, he still wasn't able to go immediately to sleep. It was like the day was re-wound and playing in his mind. Just before falling asleep, he said, "Bet I have more converts since I was assigned here than Father Morris."

Chapter 15

It was one of those mornings when the temperature was comfortable with a fresh, soothing breeze. The perfect time to open all the windows and let the air flow through the house. Father did just that, plus he opened the kitchen door. He was dressed for the Morning Mass; however, spent more time than usual listening to a mockingbird on the back deck railing mimicking many others bird calls and chirps.

On the clock over the refrigerator, he noted the time was seven fifty seven. With only three minutes before Mass he rushed to the door. Just as he pushed out the storm door he saw on his new welcome mat a black and white ball of fur.

The little fellow uncurled himself from his early morning nap. He stood with his tail wagging to peer up to Father. As a young child, Father was slightly mauled by a neighbor's dog, which caused him to fear any size dog. He pulled the storm door to and closed the door. He thought if he used the back door and rushed he could still make it on time.

Stepping up to the church's side door, he realized he forgot to bring the key and the door was locked. He turned in time to see the little fellow was headed toward him. He almost ran around to the front of the church to get in. The doors were blocked open so he walked fast down the aisle to the altar. His concentration during the Mass was difficult since the little fellow positioned himself just outside the doors as if he was waiting. Sometimes he appeared to watch and listen for awhile, and then lay down as if he was bored. He never made an attempt to come in until Communion time. Being Wednesday, only seven people were in attendance. When they rose to come forward for Communion the little fellow stood, hesitated a moment and then trotted down the aisle to fall in line. Mr. Gruder was the last in line for Communion. When he turned to leave there was no barrier between Father's feet and the dog. Father was hesitant to move. The little fellow just stood there, tail straight and eyes up to Father's...waiting. Snickers could be heard. Father was cautious as he turned to go behind the altar. The little dog watched and waited a minute before he walked to the right to Father's chair and lay down beside it.

Father closed as usual with, "The Mass is ended, go in peace." The little feller stretched out with his head on the floor but kept an eye on Father. Father rushed ahead to get outside.

"Where'd you git the pup?" Mr. Gruder asked.

Father forced a smile, "It isn't mine. He was at my door this morning. He must be lost."

"Seems to take a liking to you, he does," Mr. Gruder replied.

Big Jane came out carrying the pup in her arms, and Little Jane was reaching around to stroke his head. "He's so cute, Father. Where did you get him?"

"He's not mine. Don't know where he belongs," Father reported.

Little Jane laughed as she said, "I'd say he may not be yours, but you definitely belong to him."

Sis, Rose and the Enstruckees took turns patting his head and playing with his paws.

Big and Little Jane was the last to leave. Big Jane was careful as she handed the little feller to Father.

Alone with little feller cradled in his arms the tension began to leave. Father looked down into those deep brown eyes. His tail was lightly beating on Father's chest. Father could feel the warmth of his body as he carried him toward the rectory, and he liked the feeling. As he bent down to set him on the ground he said, "We're going to have to find your home. Wish you could talk and tell me how you got lost."

Father made a turn toward the General store to get something for breakfast. He looked back to see the dog was following a few steps behind him.

He picked him up and placed him on the porch. "Now you have to stay there while I'm gone. No dogs allowed in the store, and you could get run over."

He turned to walk away but heard the dog whine. Then the he found the steps and was right beside Father again. Twice more Father placed him on the porch and had a talk with him. The last time the little fellow was running for the steps while Father was still talking. Father's patience was tested as he stood with his hands on his hips looking down at him. "Looks like I'm gonna have to make my own breakfast," and he stepped up to the porch and into the house.

The dog positioned himself, back legs on the porch and his front on the storm door to bark and whine. After a few minutes Father opened the storm door. "Well guess you may be hungry. I'll feed you something this time, but you have to go home."

Father fried eggs and bacon to share with the little fellow. He also sat down a bowl of milk for him to drink. The dog's tail wagged as he ate, making Father chuckle. When the little feller had licked clean both the bowl and plate, he rushed to the door. Father understood he wanted out. He was pleased to open the door thinking little fellow had his tummy full, realized where his home was and wished to go to it.

He stood at the door, curious to know in which direction he would be going. The small dog ran out about twenty-five feet, did his business and headed right back to the door. It was a short standoff with Father's hand tight on the door handle and the little fellow crying and scratching to get in. Reluctantly Father opened the door to him. "Okay for now, but I'm putting a sign up in Blue's General Store and everywhere. Someone out there is looking for you."

Father went into the office to make the sign, and the little fellow curled up under one of the lamp tables for a snooze.

At the general store, Rob said, "I thought I saw someone stop in the parking lot last night and drop off something. In fact, it looked to me like they may have placed it on your porch. Think it might be your pup."

Shaking his head, Father said, "He's not my pup. To tell you the truth, I'm a little afraid of dogs."

Rob laughed, "That was yesterday. You made him breakfast. If you feed a dog he's yours. Man becomes dog's best friend."

Father relaxed to say, "But I don't know anything about a dog. I wouldn't know what to do."

Emmie Lou said, "You don't have to know anything. He'll teach you. Sounds like he already started with breakfast. What'ya gonna name him?"

"Don't know," Father smiled. "Hadn't thought about that."

Emmie Lou walked around the counter, "Here's a bag of dog food for him. You can't be cooking all the time. You're a priest...call him Deacon."

"Thanks. Maybe I'll see if he answers to that."

Father tried calling Spot, Rover, Boy, Teddy, but the little fellow only came when called Deacon or Deek.

Three days later and no one responded to any of the posters Father had placed everywhere to find his home. Tired of waiting, he made the decision to keep him. Early in the morning with Deacon in the front seat he drove to Javelle to purchase a collar, leash, dog house, posts, and fencing. A trip was made to the veterinarian for a checkup and shots. There he was told Deacon was probably about nine to ten weeks old and a small terrier breed. The veterinarian told him terriers are very active and needed lots of attention and exercise.

"All I know is that I'm certain he is much smarter than most any other dog, Father said. "Already he knows to sit, stay, sit up, dance around, fetch, and roll over."

The veterinarian smiled when he asked, "And what has he taught you?"

Father laughed, "He's very good at that, too. I know when to open the doors, give him water, feed him...he especially likes beef jerky. Then there's the quiet time when he likes to lay on his back and have his belly rubbed, or just lay on the couch with his head on my leg as I practice my sermons. Every day we've been jogging down Quaintberg Road and back. It's a little over a mile."

Handing the bill to Father, the vet said, "Smart dog."

Back at the rectory Father began an enclosure. He was careful to place the doghouse in an area that was shaded most of the day. He dug holes for the posts, set them in the concrete mix he purchased and strung the fence. He struggled with the gate, but after awhile, he was satisfied with the way it swung. All the time Deacon ran around the area sniffing, chasing grasshoppers, twice he tried digging, and barked at a squirrel in a tree. Often he took a break and tried to get Father to stop and play with him by jumping on his leg or just sitting in his way for attention.

They missed lunch, but around three that afternoon Father went in, made a sandwich and with a handful of beef jerky, selected a picnic table for a break. Father no longer talked to himself but to Deacon. It was doubted that Deacon understood most of the jargon, but always sat eye-to-eye with Father.

Occasionally he turned his head from side to side as if he understood.

The dog pen was completed. Father was ready to see if his work on the pen was successful. He walked into the pen and Deacon followed. He played with him for awhile, believing it was necessary that Deacon have get-acquainted time. First he was awarded two pieces of beef jerky for sitting and dancing around. All coaxing for him to enter the dog house failed. The next step would be to leave him in the pen with Father standing outside for security.

Problem was, each time Father started to leave, Deacon beat him to the outside. With regrets Father became forceful. He caught Deacon, placed him in the pen with the gate only slightly open and closed it fast. Deacon began to run around the pen looking for an exit. Not finding one he started to dig in an attempt to crawl under. After Father scolded him three times, Deacon stopped digging.

Deacon tried to shake the gate open. He even tried to bite through the wire. When everything failed he just sat down with his back to Father in a position Father believed to be disgust. He was not very satisfied to be placing his best friend in what could be called a qualified jail.

"No," he said out loud, "Dogs are supposed to be kept in kennels. That's not mistreatment. He's a dog."

All the time Deacon didn't move or look at him. Father couldn't take standing there any longer seeing how he believed Deacon must feel. He went into the house, but before he sat down, Deacon was scratching at the door as he often did to be let into the house.

Father opened the door and looked down at him to say, "Well, I'll be danged. Don't tell me dogs can fly. Let's go see how you got out of there."

Deacon was right at his heels as he walked around checking the fence. When he refused to go into the pen, Father picked him up and put him inside as he said, "There. Don't know how you did it, but everything looks all right to me. You just have to learn you're a dog and this is a dog kennel."

Walking back to the house, he looked back twice to see Deacon watching him go. Before he could sit down to read a book from the library about raising a dog, Deacon was again scratching and barking at the door.

He knew according to the book he had done everything right when he built the pen. Annoyed, he opened the door, picked up Deacon, walked back for the third time to place him in the kennel, but this time it would be different. His plan was after he closed the door, he would stand looking through the glass to watch how Deacon escaped.

He barely had time to close the door and pull back the curtain before Deacon showed him a trick not taught with beef jerky. Deacon could climb the fence and jump from the top.

That evening after dinner, Father sat preparing his next sermon while Deacon, as usual, lay on the couch with his head on Father's leg. Sermon completed and read to Deacon, he closed the folder. He reached down to rub Deacon's head, and said, "You would have been a big star if you'd joined a circus rather than coming to live with me. You're really smart, you know, but don't you even think about leaving me now."

Before that night, Deacon was only allowed to sleep on the rug by Father's bed.

That night he was restless and made many attempts to jump onto the bed, but his legs were too short. Father realized he forgot to say his night prayer, so he rolled out of bed and knelt down. He reached for Deacon and said, "Okay, Deek, if you're going to live with me and sleep in my bed, we must pray before we go to sleep."

He positioned Deacon with his rear on the floor, his front paws together against the mattress and began, "Now I lay me down to sleep, I pray the Lord my soul to keep. If I should die before I wake, I pray the Lord my soul to take. Plus, St. Francis, please pray for Deek and me. Amen."

Both fell asleep, but in the night Father woke. He reached around, 'til his hand touched Deacon. Deacon moved a little and made a low whimper. Father said, "Sorry, Deek, I was just making sure you're still with me."

Chapter 16

Father Bill was anxious as he sat at his table waiting for Hawk and Marg to arrive for their appointment with him. He couldn't imagine, since neither was Catholic as far as he knew, why they wished the meeting.

Exactly at six, he saw Marg's car stop in his drive. Deek rushed to the door to greet them. Father didn't rise immediately from the table. Instead, he watched them searching for any clue for their visit.

Before the doorbell rang, Deek was barking in anticipation of a friendly visitor who would rub his head and possibly give him a treat. He liked Ron the best because he always brought him peanut butter treats. Big Jane came in second since she never failed to pick him up, tickle his belly with her long finger nails and kiss him.

Following the greetings, Father invited them to sit at the table with him, and poured glasses of his sweetened mint tea.

The small talk ended when Father said, "I'm pleased you came to visit me; however, I have the feeling you've some unusual news or request."

"True," Marg began. "Hawk and I have given this a lot of thought. We have a good number of Hispanics working at Wright Farm. Many are here only for a period of time when needed for the crops. They have work permits. A few are legal full-time employees. You've met Juan and Rosetta."

Father nodded, "Yes. Rosetta, but I only saw Juan."

Hawk spoke up, "The good news is that Juan was found guilty for participating in Lawrence's death, but due to circumstances of the serious threats from Earl Sneakel, he'll not serve time in jail. He'll be on probation for five years. Juan's really a good man. I know, it would be hard for you to believe, but he's a very good family man. He would do anything for Rosetta and his daughter, Juanita. Anything—and the judge believed him."

Marg broke in, "Yes, my lawyer was able to get the judge to listen to the whole truth of what happened between he, Earl and Bee. He was exiled to Mexico by Lawrence when he learned Bee was expecting a baby by Juan. In Mexico he worked any job he could get until he could get back into the USA legally. That man even became an American citizen before he returned to Wright Farm to be with his wife and daughter."

"True," Hawk joined in, "they work for us, but they're like my family. Rosetta totally runs the house operation. Juan supervises the care of the yard and gardens. He has a wealth of knowledge about grass, shrubs, flowers, trees, and keeps reading books about them. For that, I'll give Bee credit. She was his educator, teaching him to speak correctly, and to read and write."

Marg smiled as she added, "Their girl, Juanita—she's special. Smart and sings like an angel. Taught herself to play the piano. Plays by ear."

Father wished to get to the reason for their visit and asked, "That's all good, but why are you coming to me?"

Marg and Hawk looked at each other before Marg began, "Hawk and I want our people to be comfortable while they work for us. We always give them Sundays off, but they don't have a church to attend. We believe most are Catholic. They gather in a group on Sunday mornings and pray together. Neither of us speaks Spanish, and, of course, all their prayers are in Spanish. Rosetta told me she would like to attend Mass every Sunday, and so would most of the others. Would you accept them?"

The surprise silenced Father for a moment. To give it more thought, he got up and went for the pitcher to pour more tea. Glasses full, he sat back down to say, "Sure, they're welcome; however, our Masses are in English. I speak maybe ten or twelve words in Spanish. A number of them aren't fit for mixed company. Learned them one summer when I volunteered to be a camp councilor at a mission in Texas for underprivileged boys. I had no idea what they were saying about me until one of the boys did the translation. To get respect, I knocked some heads together. I couldn't believe it when they begged for me to come back the next year. Still no 'Espinol.' He stood. "Let me give it some thought. Yes, I would like to have them attend. Problem is, they may not feel comfortable here. I'll get back to you."

He wrestled with his thoughts long into the night and all the next day. There was no doubt in his mind that he was to minister to all cultures. To mesh European Americans with Spanish would be a challenge. He remembered stories about his ancestors back in the eighteen hundreds when the Irish were brought to America to build the railroads. His family settled west of St. Louis at the time. St. Joseph Parish of Manchester was their church. In the 1860's, German immigrants began to move to that area. They too were Catholic. There was no trust. The conflict was so bad each kept their own books and never attended the same Mass for a couple of generations. Father was born in Dogtown, an Irish settlement within the city of St. Louis. Just across the highway from Dogtown was St. Ambrose Parish for the Italians. It was the same with them and it was a couple generations before the Irish and the Italians began to have civil relationships. Now he was seeing himself to be the center of another conflict of cultures.

Decision made, he phoned members to attend a meeting in his basement to attack the problem. Ruth Enstruckee was always dependable. He placed a call for her and her husband, George, to attend. Ron Goodman was elected president of the Men's Club, so he and Big Jane were invited. Wilber Freehil was doing a great job working with children. He thought his input would be helpful, and placed that call. Knowing Big and Little Jane were always together; he chose not to split the pair and invited the Shorts. The Mexican attendance could impact the general store, so Rob and Emmie Lou were invited. The last three selected were Rose, Sis, and Mr. Gruder, who were his favorites when he had the need to bounce idea off others.

No one was told why they were to attend. A shock of silence came when he stood and announced, "A few nights ago I had a visit from Hawk Wright and Marg Wright. They came to ask if the Mexicans at Wright Farm would be welcome to attend Mass here. I've brought you together to assist me in making preparations for that. I would like your opinions and suggestions."

Sis's hand went up first and without recognition began, "Why do they want to dump them on us? They got plenty of money. Let 'em build their own church."

Mr. Gruder never raised his hand. "Dad-burn, Sis's right. My ol' mother always said, 'ever tub must sit on its own bottom'. She be right. We no need to be taken 'em in."

Rob called from the back, "They got no money. Wont be botherin' us none."

"That Marg," Big Jane said, I don't like her. You should tell her to go back East."

"That Hawk," Little Jane's said, "he's not Catholic. He's Indian. Don't know what they are."

Both Ron and Wilber stood. The silence was broken when Ron said, "You go first, Wilber."

Wilber shook his head, "No, Ron, I think you were up first. Go ahead."

Ron's voice was firm as he began, "Now I'm not Catholic and don't understand you guys. I don't think you've thought this out. These are, as you call yourselves, God's people. Just like you and me. Hawk only came to speak for them. You sound like you only want this church to be for white people. I know you. You don't really mean that. You know God's people come in all colors...black, yellow, red, and white. Now calm down and let's put our heads together for a solution." As he sat down he added, "Now go ahead, Wilber."

Wilber applauded alone for a few seconds before others joined him. "I was about to say almost the same thing, but I think Ron put it into words we all understand. We shouldn't make the same mistakes our ancestors did when they came as immigrants to America. Learn from history. I, as you know, like Ron, am not Catholic, but I love this community. It's growing and growing fast. Father has called us here to work with him. I'd like to hear some constructive ideas."

Rose held up her hand.

"Yes, Rose," Father said.

Rose with her normal soft tones asked, "What if we invited them to Mass and prepared a lunch afterward in the hall to get to know them?"

Father replied, "That would be fine, Rose, but there is a problem. Most of these people don't speak English or very little English. I don't speak Spanish. To talk with one of them, I would need a translator. I don't know how much those people would get from our Mass, yet if they choose to come, we should welcome them. Yes, Ruth?"

Ruth smiled as she volunteered, "George and I both speak a little Spanish. Just about enough when we go to Mexico we can get by. I'd be willing to try and teach them a little English if they would choose to remain after Mass. George could help me."

George stood to join her. "I understand that a man who owns a small company that makes skids is considering moving his company to this area because of the availability of timber. I was told most of his employees are Mexicans."

Rob jumped up. "There you go. They're coming over here taking our jobs. If that happens we're goin' to have more of 'em."

Emmie Lou stood beside him to say, "Wait a minute, Rob. That makes good sense to me. We need cheap skids to ship to keep the costs down. They must be cheap. I bet you couldn't find a man around here to work at that for the price they pay. That's totally unskilled labor. Our county needs a better tax base. I say bring 'em on in. Then get us a company here that makes items to ship on skids that needs skilled labor. That'll be progress."

Kate's hand went up and Father called on her. "Father, it sounds like I'm for segregation but at this time it might be right. Why not have a separate Mass for them? Maybe one of them who speak enough English could do some translation.

Father liked the idea and said, "You know, Kate that just might be the answer. I've been thinking, possibly there's a priest in the Archdiocese who speaks Spanish. He could be assigned here. I'd hate to go, but it might be worked out. I could..."

"Ohs!" cut him off and Big Jane jumped up to say, "That ain't gonna happen. You're not leaving us. We'll all go to St. Louis in protest if we have to. Forget that!"

Father's smile was wide when he said, "Now, I thank all of you for coming. I'm going to give the separate Mass some thought. It could be a starter. You all know our great pitcher, Stone. He might work as the translator for me."

"You think he knows enough Spanish to do that? Sis asked. He's such a good kid. He might if you ask him."

Father wanted to be kind when he remarked, "Sis, I think you forgot, Spanish is his first language. He's Mexican and Indian. See how easy it is to mesh with persons of different background. You don't see his color, you see his goodness."

Mr. Gruder had the last words before the meeting came to a close. "His Dad, him good feller too. Him do most work at market anymore. Maybe some more good ones. We'll 'ave ta just see."

Deek found his first good one when Hawk and Marg brought Juanita, Juan, and Rosetta to meet with Father. Juanita immediately picked him up to play. He had her undivided attention all the time the adults were meeting.

Stone had arrived early and followed them into the kitchen where extra folding chairs were set.

Father began by reintroducing Stone to the others, and then stated, "I've given your request for the Mexicans to attend Mass here at St. Francis a lot of thought. We would be most happy to have the workers at Wright Farm join our Parish. For those who do not understand English, I'll have a separate Mass for them. Stone here will do the translating. He and I are going to work that out. After the first Mass, for the new members of the parish, a few are going to prepare a luncheon for them in the hall."

Marg spoke up, "Oh, I'll pay for that...the food and their time. That would really be appreciated."

"No. No." Father shook his head. It'll be their gift to the new members of our Parish. One couple has volunteered to have a class after Mass for those interested in learning English. That may come later if they wish. Time wise, I think, possibly a Mass at eleven-thirty would be all right. We have a Mass at seven and nine so I can add the eleven-thirty to my schedule. How does that sound to you?"

"It would be fine," Hawk replied. We have a bus to bring them. Juan is a good driver, and sometimes I may bring them myself. I know nothing about your religion, but would like to learn."

Marg questioned, "It doesn't matter, but what is the cost for your service? I'm willing to pay for it—whatever it is. "

Father laughed, "The right to worship in our country is free. Normally at our Mass we take a collection to pay for the expenses of the parish; however, in this case I know your people have little money. We won't be doing that at their Mass."

Marg was insistent saying, "I'll pay for them. How much is it?"

Still smiling Father stood, "I'll send you a bill once a month," he joked. "I know where you live."

They rose to their feet. Marg looked at Father as she smiled, and said, "I get it. I'm beginning to realize priests don't always tell the truth. You're not going to send me a bill. If I do get one, I'm going to come here with Hawk to see if it's worth my money."

Father didn't let that one slip by. "In that case, I'll be sending a bill. It'll be a large amount to make sure you get here."

The first Mass for the Mexicans went well. Stone did the translating except for the Lord's Prayer. That was Father's first accomplishment to learn Spanish. He stood proud as he began:

"Padre nuestro que est'as en los cielos
Santificado sea tu Nombre
Venga tu reino
H'agase tu voluntad
En la tierra como en el cielo
Danos hoy el pan de este dia
y perdona nuestras deudas
como nosotros perdonamos neustros deudores
y no nos dejes caer en al tentaci'on
sino que libranos del malo. Amen."

The luncheon afterward was a big success. The women were surprised when Marg Wright came into the kitchen wearing no jewelry, little make-up, a simple dress and flat shoes. Smiling, she made the request for someone to give her a job. She took napkins from Rose and chatted with the other workers as she placed them on the tables. When everyone was served the workers moved about the dining area to find a seat at a table to be able to eat with the Mexicans. Although, in most all cases communications were limited to smiles and nods.

A real treat was when Stone encouraged Juanita to play the piano, so he and she could sing Spanish songs together. The one exception was Big Jane's request for 'South of the Border'.

If there was any disappointment it was Father's and Mrs. Olheimer's. Together they often talked about Stone becoming a priest and prayed for him. It was obvious to them that his eyes kept mostly turned to Juanita. Deek, too, soon realized the attention he wished from Juanita was being stolen by Stone.

Deek wandered around the hall getting tidbits of food until Big Jane came from the kitchen to cradle him in her arms.

As they left, there many gracias heard and several hugs. The working ladies enjoyed the luncheon so much, it was decided they would serve one once a month for the new parishioners.

When Cinco de Mayo Day came, the surprise was for the European Americans.

Everyone was invited to the hall to celebrate with the Mexicans at two in the afternoon.

Mexican women, a few dressed in traditional costumes, served tacos, enchiladas, salsa, and tortilla chips. The decorations were red, white and green to represent the Mexican flag. There was soda, tea, and Mexican beers to drink while Mariachi Bands serenaded. After a few beers and tons of laughter a few attempted to learn the Mexican Hat Dance. That night, Juanita closed her diary after writing the last line, 'a good time was had by all'.

Chapter 17

It was a mid-October night when Big Jane and Ron had Father Bill, Little Jane, and John Short to dinner. The pork roast and veggies were good. For dessert Big Jane served her fresh baked apple dumplings. Everyone's tummy was overstuffed as no one ever left a good-size crumb on their plate when Big Jane cooked.

The men retired to the patio with full glasses of Quaintberg wine leaving the women to do the dishes. Ron started a fire in the fire-pit to take away the slight chill of the night. Dishes washed, dried and put away, the women joined them.

Sitting down with her glass of wine, Big Jane said, "Can't hardly believe this is an October night when the temperature is about 60 or 65 degrees. Better enjoy it because it's not going to last. Jack Frost has been on the pumpkin a few times already."

"A perfect night with the big harvest moon," Little Jane added. "Course a full moon is when the crazies come out."

Off in the distance they could hear 'Bob-white, bob white.' Down at the pond frogs were croaking. Now and then came a hoot from the hoot owl.

An eerie, high-pitched sound caused Father to sit up, and ask, "Where is that coming from? Sounded like a woman in trouble."

Ron gave a belly-laugh, and said, "Father, that's a screech owl. Does sound that way, though."

"You're still a city boy," John said, "guess you like honking horns, squealing tires, and sirens. I couldn't take 'em. If you stick around here very long you may never want to go back to the city."

Father held up his glass to say, "Here's to country living. Love it, but still a lot to learn."

John turned to Ron. "Suppose he's ever been snipe hunting?"

Big Jane was serious when she said, "Now don't you boys even think of doing that! Father, it's a trick they play on guys who know little about the country. Don't go with them."

Ron grinned when he said, "We'd never do that to him." There was a pause and then he spoke again. "I like watching an occasional cloud moving across the moon to dim the light for a time. Look! That one passing now almost looks like a witch with a long nose and her long dress dragging behind. Watch...after she passes, the moonlight will shine bright through the trees out there. Together, the moonlight casting shadows and the breeze swaying the tree limbs makes a weird dance on the ground."

All eyes turned toward the nearby woods. John with a hushed, low-key voice said, "Tell me if you see that big ol' wolf out there in them woods again.'Bout the time of night they go on the prowl. We'd better watch out for him."

"Have you really seen a wolf?" Father asked. "Are they in this part of the country?"

"Not normally," John said, "but occasionally one will be reported. Ron and Jane saw one a couple weeks ago. I've not seen one since I was a boy. There are lots of fox, coyotes, and a few bobcats. Wolves have to be pretty hungry to be near humans. Better watch Deek. They'll even go after adult men when there's little else for them to eat. Jane's dad's neighbor was mauled by two a number of years ago. He was lucky to escape."

Father smirked as he asked, "Jane is this another got-ya story told to city boys?"

She rose to get another bottle of wine, but said, "No, Father. That's for real. What bothered me was the one here was a black wolf. They're the worst. When Ron started into the house to get his gun, he just left me standing out here. Think he may have been using me for bait, hoping to get a better shot. I rushed right after him, but didn't talk to him for a couple hours."

Father turned to Ron, "You didn't shoot him?"

"No, Father. He ran when I opened the back door. Don't know how smart they are. He wouldn't leave when I threw a piece of wood and couple rocks at him, but guess he saw the gun."

Everyone's glass was filled again. Ron poked the fire and added another log. Little Jane spoke, "On the way over, John and I were talking about projects to make money for the church. He mentioned it being Halloween time, maybe we could decorate the hall to be haunted and charge admission."

Big Jane threw up her hands and said, "Ha! Ron there's your chance! Rent them your haunted house. They won't even have to have anyone dressed up as ghosts since the ghosts are already in there."

John sat up straight, "I forgot about that place. Ron, have you rented it again?"

Ron was slightly embarrassed and sat quiet, but Big Jane answered, "Not after the third one moved out about a year ago. They stayed two nights."

Sparks flew up from the fire when Little Jane poked around in it with a stick. "I'm not going down there. Never again. When I was a teenager, four of us started to walk down there. We were almost to the bottom of the hill when we saw the round light coming toward us. Never ran so fast in all my life. Count me out."

Big Jane crossed her arms before she said, "You'd have to be crazy to go. Ron should burn that old place down...barn, chicken house, and all. That's the reason I didn't want us to buy this place. All these years and I've never gone down there. If that damn light ever comes up here, I'm gone."

Father sat listening for a time and then asked, "Is this another story or are you really afraid there could be some paranormal activity around it? Where is it?"

Wanting to try to set the story straight, Ron explained, "This up here is about five acres and then it drops down to a little valley where there's a spring that starts around a wet creek. In the springtime it's really pretty down there. I picked it up at an auction...all thirty-seven acres. This house here and that one down there.

"Ol' Man Thevil lived down there and raised goats. Them goats stripped that far hillside so clean nothing much has ever grown back. It sat empty for a long time and then Claude Brown bought it and built this house. That was just before the war. He was killed in the war."

A smile creased Father's face, "So you think Claude Brown is your ghost?"

"Oh, no," Big Jane said, "I might not be afraid of him. It's that Ol' Thevel Goat Man, killing all those women and burying them in the cellar under the house."

"I still shiver when I think about it," Little Jane said. "That first mail-order bride may have died, but the autopsy showed he broke the neck of the second. It's believed he needed money and went to take out an insurance policy on the third. She would have to go to the insurance office to sign. Couldn't. She was already dead. Enough arsenic in her to kill three women. I just bet they were the ones who drove him to the creek and held him 'til he drowned."

A cackle of laughter came from Ron, "You girls are all crazy. Imagining stuff all the time. I go down there and nothing bothers me. Sure, I hear noises and all, but it doesn't bother me. Father, you don't believe in ghosts?"

What he knew, he was not sure he should impart and sat silent.

John broke the silence, "Well, maybe I do. Maybe, no. I'm not sure. I think if I don't bother them, they won't bother me. I don't like to go around places like that. Father, you didn't answer."

Father sat up with legs outstretched and crossed them. "There's nothing in the scriptures about situations like that, but some believe what you're calling ghosts are lost souls. They're between earth and eternity."

"Hell," Big Jane said, "that's where he belongs. Double Hell if there is such a thing."

"You gotta' be kidding?" Ron said.

Father shook his head and attempted to explain to Ron. "Many people, both Catholic and non-Catholic, call the Archdiocese every year about paranormal activities in their homes. Their stories vary. Some will say they saw a misty object and others think they see a solid figure. A few in a room may see the same thing at the same time while others see nothing. The round lights are called orbs and it's thought to be a form of energy. Often these are captured in photographs—one, two, or many. One theory is that the lost souls are attempting to get your attention for prayers so they can move on to eternity. Usually they don't hurt you; however, if you were to annoy one, they could become bad."

John could no longer sit quiet. "So there are ghosts. You believe that?"

A serious thought was to not admit his feelings so he responded, "Possibly. I have no experience with them. If I were to encounter one, I doubt I'd be afraid."

"What would you do?" John asked.

"I'd treat it as I would any stranger," Father said, "I'd probably ask his name or what did he want. Maybe ask why he's contacting me. Really don't know. Don't think I'll ever see or hear one."

Ron stood, "Father, how about you and me going down to the old house so you can see what they're talking about? Maybe they'd believe you when you return without a ghost. I'll go get some strong flashlights. John, wanna come with us?"

Big Jane sat erect, "And, Father, if you see one, do me a favor and tell him to go on to wherever. Don't you dare bring him up here! What do they call that...exorcism?"

Ron returned with three flashlights, so everybody would have one. As they headed for the overgrown lane to go down the hill, Ron called back, "Girls, while we're gone, you can go into the closet where Jane had that new dressing mirror installed. Close the door and call-up Bloody Mary."

Big Jane yelled back, "Okay Ron! You keep poking fun at my mirror you'll be bunking with Ol' Dude."

With her arms hugging her, Little Jane said, "I'd never go in there and close the door. Suppose the electricity went off when you're in there with that big mirror?"

About halfway down the hill, John slipped on a rock causing his feet to go forward, and he sat hard on the ground. "Damn!" he spurted. "Almost spilled my wine."

"You okay?" Ron called back.

Halfway to standing position John yelled, "Hey, fellers! Did you see that?"

Stopping to look back, Father asked, "See what? I didn't see anything."

Ron had walked back to see that John was all right. "You sure you're all right?"

John stood but didn't move forward. He told them about the round light he saw for just a few seconds down near the barn. "It wasn't very big, but I did see it. Think it must'a gone inside somewhere."

Ron turned back to continue down the steep hill and said, "John, I guess a fall like that could knock the daylights out of you. There's no light down there. Come on. Walk carefully."

Father stopped and stated, "There. There it is. What could it be?"

"Now you are getting like John," Ron chuckled. "It's probably just the moonlight shining on something. You guys spook easily."

Slightly embarrassed Father admitted, "You're probably right. I did think I saw a light bouncing around for just a moment or two."

The lane curved to the right. As they passed the leaning old barn there was a fluttering noise causing John and Father to stop in their tracks. "What's that?" John whispered.

Again Ron laughed. "Some pigeons have taken to roosting here. We must have scared them."

Everyone heard the bang!

Father, in an attempt to be calm, said, "Guess that was them closing the door when they left."

Ron, who was leading, stopped and turned back to say, "Now that I can't explain. Must have been the wind or something."

John stood still and said, "I don't feel any wind. Are you sure?"

Ron's voice was not friendly when he said, "Maybe I should have left you back at the house with the girls. There are no ghosts down here."

Standing and looking toward the house, John asked, "You did bring the key? I'd hate to walk back down here again in the dark."

"Now that's the funny part," Ron explained. "Yeah, I have the key, but most of the time I don't need it. The door will be unlocked and sometimes standing wide open. Ol' Dude won't come down here anymore. A couple times I've thrown him in the back of the pickup truck. We almost get to the barn when he jumps out and runs back up to the house. Deek seems to stay close to you, Father."

Father's voice was proud when he said, "Deek. I think he thinks he's a Rottweiler. He's not afraid of anything. He's probably sticking close to protect me."

"What's that? That sound?" John whispered. "Sounds like running water."

Ron was a little annoyed with John's skepticism. "I told you, there's a creek down here. It's the water rippling over the rocks."

Quieter yet, John said, "I don't hear it now. Do you?"

"Didn't someone say they drowned the old guy in the creek?" Father asked.

"Yes," Ron said. "Don't know who did it. The sheriff didn't do much investigating after they found the women's bodies in the cellar. Guess he thought justice was served."

"That or the spirits ran him away," John added. "I don't think the sheriff ever came back after they removed Ol' Thevil's body from the creek. It was only about a quarter of a mile from here. Funny how that old fortune teller called the sheriff's office to say she saw graves under this ol' house. All the time they'd been wondering where the women went."

Ron turned back toward the house. "Father, some of the furniture's still in the house or maybe all of it. You've heard about a picture of a person whose eyes follow you around a room? Darn, if there isn't one here just like that. Come on. I'll show it to you."

When they stepped up on the porch, Ron turned his flashlight toward the door and it swung open a bit.

"That's scary," John whispered. "I thought I saw that door move."

Ron turned back to him, "You did. Guess the foundation is about rotted out. Our weight must have tilted the house to cause the door to move."

His voice was a little shaky when John said, "You fellers go on in. I have so many allergies—don't want to be sick. I know there's a lot of dust in there. I'll wait right here."

"Go ahead," Ron said, "but hold tight to one of these posts. I don't want to come back out here and find the haunts drug you off."

"Seriously," John said, "I have allergies."

A heavy cloud blanketed the moon plunging the little valley to total darkness. The breeze stopped, almost sucking away the air as Father and Ron, with Deek in the lead, entered the living room. Deek immediately began sniffing around. With his flashlight Ron showed Father the picture of the sinister-looking man whose eyes followed a person across the room. "Isn't that neat?" Ron asked. Although they were in the dark with the flashlights on the picture, the man in the picture glared at them.

"I've got an idea," Father suggested. "Let's test him. Let's part ways. You go over there and I'll move over here. See who he watches."

They took the positions and Ron said, "He's looking at me."

Father reported, "Can't be. He's looking at me."

"How do you suppose he can do that?" Ron asked.

"That has to be a painting by a fine artist to make eyes like that," Father said. "Have any idea who that man is in the picture?"

Meantime Deek had ventured back into the kitchen, sniffing, and farther back into the screened porch where that door stood open as well.

All of a sudden, Deek gave out a piercing I'm-going-to-be-killed, yell. His little legs dug and slid on the old linoleum as he made the mad dash through the house and out the front door. He didn't stop at John, but ran halfway up the lane.

Father and Ron's flashlight-beams followed him as he scrambled out the door. They turned toward each other. Father glimpsed Ron's white face and figured his matched. Then came sounds they figured must be coming up from the bowels of Hell. Hooves beat and scuffed the floor. Things moved about. Pots and pans banged together. Dishes were broken. In the dark, something large fell. Another bang and something slid across the floor.

Father and Ron leaped for the door. They almost wedged themselves in, trying to get away. John heard the noise and didn't stop until he was well away from the house. In no time flat, Father and Ron gathered at his side.

Secretly, each wondered if they were far enough away to be safe. Somehow their flashlights were turned off in the turmoil. It was a few moments before Ron dared to turn his flashlight back on to point the beam toward the front door. What a shocker it was when in the light they saw a herd of goats in the living room window. In the door stood a big horned, dark brown billy goat with a long white beard. Ol' Billy gave his call, "Baaaaa. Baaaaa!"

It was uncontrollable laughter from all when Father announced, "Exorcism complete."

Chapter 18

Deek heard the sound of a truck before Father, and came running around from the back of the house to see who it was. Father watched a brand new 1948 black Ford pickup truck as it turned into his drive. He stopped the swing when he recognized Ron Goodman, and stood.

As Ron got out of the truck, Father called, "They must pay good down there where you're working. That's a good looking truck."

Ron, being his jolly good self, was smiling as he headed to the porch. "Got it this morning. Marg Wright bought my old one. She and Hawk came to get it last night." With his hand on the storm-door handle, he reached down to rub Deek's head, and said, "Father, you teach him how to do all kinds of stuff. How about teaching him to bring me a beer?"

Father chuckled as he sat back down, "Can't do that, Ron. You'll have to go get it yourself. It would be illegal. He's not old enough to serve alcohol."

Ron returned from the kitchen, and sat beside Father in the swing. "Boy, they have loads of stuff planned there at Wright Farm. We'll be working there for years. First they're building three new houses for their—I guess you'd call them servants. I know one is for Juan and Rosetta, one is for the chauffeur's family and don't know about the third. The old quarters will be rehabbed for guests. Then they're clearing that property facing PP. You know they donated 16 acres to the hospital in Poplar Bluff. Even gave them enough money to build a medical center. It'll be called The Lawrence Wright Medical Center. They're also cutting straight through the woods to make a two lane paved road directly to Wright Farm. Doing all kinds of stuff. Hope the money don't run out."

Father assured Ron, "I don't believe you need worry about that. Since Marg and Hawk went east and got married, they're making all kind of changes. He told me this'll be their permanent home. She sold one company and resigned as president of the other, but will remain Chairman of the Board. She's on the board of a couple other corporations. Her house in New Jersey is for sale. They'll keep her apartment in New York. Hope it goes well for them, but I find it hard to believe she's going to adjust to the country life. She doesn't appear to be the type."

"That does beat all," Ron stated "but look at you. Don't think you've been back to St. Louis since you came. Couldn't believe it...last night when Jane told Marg, she, Little Jane, and Kate were going to see a show in Poplar Bluff, Marge asked if she could join them. She was already at the house when I left. Dressed about like the other girls."

"Guess you know, they've completed their instruction to become Catholic?" Father asked. "Hawk said, after they're baptized they want to be married in the church and have a small private celebration. I'll be busy for awhile doing baptizing. Stone is ready and there are two new babies in the area."

There was silence for a minute or two before Ron stopped the swinging by stretching his legs out and looked down at his feet.

Father took note of his unusual actions, and asked, "You didn't come here to talk about the Wrights, did you? Is there something wrong?"

Ron didn't look up, but sat stiff except for turning his beer bottle around a couple times. He voice was low but clear when he announced, "I want to be baptized Catholic."

Father exclaimed, "Ron! Are you all right? Is there something wrong with you?"

Ron shook his head as he looked in Father's face.

Father was still confused and asked, "What happened?"

Ron's voice was almost quivering when he replied, "Oh, physically I'm okay. I've just been giving it a lot of thought. You know I'm around here doing stuff all the time. I—I like it. I guess it's like this...I think if you're going to play on the team, you should wear the uniform."

Father jumped to his feet, grabbed Ron's hand in the excitement, and declared, "This is such a wonderful surprise. I'm so happy. You stay right here. I'm going to get both of us a beer. When I come back, we can make plans."

Wilber Freehill and John Short joined Ron at his kitchen table to play cards while they waited for the girls to return from the show.

John spoke up, "You're really going to shock Jane when you tell her you're going to become Catholic. Do it while I'm here. I want to see her face."

Wilber cleared his throat, and slowly asked, "You're really going to do it, aren't you?"

Ron smiled, laying down a full hand, "You bet I am. Father wants to wait to talk with Jane before we pick a date. Looks like my lucky day. Can anyone beat a full house...Jacks over sevens?"

Wilber cleared his throat again before beginning, "You're right. We are almost Catholic—volunteering all the time like Catholics."

Picking up the cards to shuffle, John said, "You can't get all the credit for that. Them girls feel free to volunteer us for everything. It's like they think we have strong backs and weak minds."

Ron laughed, but noticed Wilber was deep in thought. His dealt cards were left lying on the table. Ron and John looked at each other and both turned to Wilber. John asked, "Ain't that right Wilber?"

Wilber just moved his cards around, then began to speak, "I've give this some thought, too. Ron, you reckon he'd do us both at the same time?"

Ron was tickled, and replied, "Guess he would, as long as we don't demand he change the water after the first one. You'd really do it with me?"

Before he could reply the door opened, and the four girls walked into the kitchen.

The guys got up as John said, "There's four of 'em. Better pull out a fourth chair. Here, Marg, you take my chair."

The guys were actually giddy as they insisted the girls sit down and listen.

Kate looked up, "You guys been drinking—or up to something? What's so funny?"

"Have we got a surprise for you!" John couldn't wait any longer. Ron and Wilber are going to be baptized! Ron already talked with Father Bill about it. Isn't that great?"

The stunned expressions on their faces were priceless for the guys. Big Jane blurted out, "You gotta be kidding! Ron, you didn't do that?"

Standing square with his hands in his pockets, Ron said, "Went to talk with Father right after you left. He said I'd only need a little instruction, since I've been around the church and Catholics so long. Figure it would be the same for Wilber."

Big Jane began to laugh, "Ron, if this is true, he should have taken you right away and dunked your head in that baptismal fountain. You'll be by him like you are with me. You say you're not going to stop drinking beer on Friday nights with the guys. Maybe you don't drink more, but you never drink less." She turned to Marg. "Marg, that's how your pickup truck got all those dents. Fortunately, he never ran into anything more than the ditch, a fence post, or once a tree. If he does that to the new truck, I'm gonna dent him."

John was laughing uncontrollably and burst out, "I'll never forget the time we had to work on a Saturday after he came home late on a Friday night. That Saturday at noon, we all sat down to open our lunch boxes. The expression on his face was so funny. He'd been too sick to eat his dinner when he got home that Friday night. When he opened his lunch box on Saturday, Jane had scraped all his dinner into it and put a note on top. It read, 'Dear, you don't like me wasting anything, so here's your dinner you didn't eat last night.'"

Marg shook her head in disbelief, "You didn't!"

Little Jane cackled, "Oh, yes she did! Jane tell her about the times he would come home from drinking and be sick...what you did one time with the diaper."

Big Jane was enjoying the attention. "Every Friday night he'd go to the bar to get his check cashed. Then he'd start drinking with the boys. He couldn't drink much back then. He'd come home and run for the bathroom because he was sick. Usually he'd sit down on the floor with his long legs wrapped around the toilet bowl. Well, one time, I got tired of checking on him, so I put a pillow on the side of the bathtub for him to lay his head on, and tied his arms around the commode with one of Jack's diapers, so he couldn't fall backwards.

Figured he'd be all right, so I went to bed. I hardly got off to sleep before he began to yell."

Everyone was laughing at Ron's expense until Marg interrupted, "I've an idea. Hawk and I have finished our instructions—ready for baptism. Let's ask Father if he could baptize all of us at the same time. We could have a little lunch celebration afterward. Either everyone bring a dish, or we have it catered."

"Good idea!" Both Janes exclaimed.

Kate bounced right up with, "Like the catering idea, or we could all go to Big Al's Steak House."

Rising and waving her hands, Big Jane suggested, "Let's go into the living room and make plans. Marg, that's a wonderful idea. Come on!"

The guys sat back down, picked up their hands and began to play cards again.

Wilber was the first to speak. "Looks like all we'll have to do is show up. They'll take care of the rest. I was watching Kate. Couldn't read her mind to see what she was really thinking."

"I got it at the end," John said. "I know what they're thinking. Another good reason to eat out."

The second Saturday of the next month was chosen for the baptisms. At two in the afternoon everyone arrived with their families for the affair. Babies were first, followed by Stone. Stone was dressed in a light blue sport coat and black slacks. Mr. Olheimer insisted Stone wear one of his neckties. Pablo was very handsome in his new navy blue suit purchased by the Olheimers for his birthday.

Stone's deep brown eyes gleamed as he stepped forward to be baptized. He reached into his pocket, found the heart shaped locket with his mother's picture, and held it tight in his hand. As soon as he was baptized, he held it up for his father to see. Pablo grabbed him to give him a big hug. Then Stone was hugged and kissed by Mrs. Olhemer. Everyone stepped up to shake his hand, but his brown-skin face flushed red when Juanita took his hand and kissed his cheek.

After Father baptized Wilber, Ron was next. Baptisms compete Father turned back to get the cover for the fountain. Turning back around, he saw Juanita and Stone standing before him. In Stone's arms was a wiggly Deek who wanted no part of being baptized. Father stuck his hand in the water and flecked droplets toward the three of them. "Go in peace now, and get him out of here."

The Ladies Solidity took charge to decorate the hall. A cake was to be delivered from the Jasper Bakery. The plans were to serve coffee, tea and soda; however, Mr. Gruder did not believe it to be a celebration unless his wine was chilled and served, too.

Kate and Big Jane struggled to act as if it were just another day, but inside their hearts were dancing. Once off to themselves, they grabbed each other as tears rolled down their cheeks. Big Jane said, "I didn't think I'd ever see this day. I'm so happy."

"Me, too," said Kate as she leaned back and rubbed a tear from Big Jane's cheek.

Father accidentally walked around the corner to see them. With a smile, he advised, "Better not get to gushy, girls, or they may not take you to Big John's Steak House. Ron, John, Hawk and Wilber, all said they would buy my dinner. I'm going to eat one and ask for rain-checks for the other three."

Chapter 19

Hawk was extremely concerned as he sat on the couch in the rectory to talk with Father. "I think had I known what would happen, I'd never have hired that black woman. None of this makes sense. Do you think I should let her go? Would that quieten things down?"

"Hold on, Hawk," Father interrupted."That would be wrong. This is not your fault. It would have been wrong if you didn't hire her because of her color or sex. Let her go? Only if she's not qualified for the job. I've been curious as to how you came to hire her."

"Well, there's a lot of property to clear for the new medical building." Hawk said with a smile. Also, I want to clear the acreage all the way back to our compound so it's not hidden as if we are doing something illegal. It'll be cleared and then landscaped properly. All in all, we have many, many acres to clear. I wasn't expecting a woman to apply when I ran the ad for an engineer to supervise the project. I received three resumes for the position. Two men and Fanny Ruff. Reading Fanny's resume I knew, if it were true, she was the better candidate, but I preferred to talk with the men.

"Marg saw the resume on my desk, and insisted I interview her. After checking all her references, I made the call to set an appointment for the interview. At two, on the day she was to arrive, she was a no-show. Knowing she was coming from St. Louis, I waited in the office for another thirty minutes. Then I told Dori, my secretary, I was going back into the woods to check with the surveying team.

It was a little after three when I heard a woman's voice call, 'Mr. Wright? Mr. Wright? Where are you?' I suspected it was her and hollered back, 'I'm over here near the fence. I can see you. I'm waving. Can you see me?' She replied, and started toward me. Separating us was a big mud-hole about five feet across and maybe ten to twelve feet long. When she reached it she stopped to ask, 'Mr. Wright? and I responded, 'Yes. Come over here. I have some questions for you'. I couldn't believe what she did. She never even pulled up her pant legs and only glanced at the mud. She walked proud right through it and up to me to ask, 'What questions do you have for me, Sir?' Having checked her references, and seeing her without hesitation walk through that mud, I stated, "I only have one. When will you be available to start working?'"

"I'd say she's got spunk," Father said. "A good story. She was only here a week or so before trouble began."

Sadly shaking his head Hawk continued, "Yes, she asked for three weeks before she reported to work. She wanted to give two weeks' notice where she worked. Then she wanted a week to find a place to live and move with her two teenage sons. Father, Mexicans have been employed at Wright Farm for many years with no trouble. A few families live here year around. Their children go into Sallow to school. I don't understand how one good black family is not accepted. There are few Indians living here. Mostly Cherokee. I'm half Arapaho. It's crazy."

Father stood to walk toward the kitchen. He turned and stopped to look out the window before turning to Hawk. "The Shorts are angry about the damage they did to their property, and mentioned it may be the KKK. I doubt it. I'd think it's more likely a gang of men who are doing all this. If it was the Klan, as I understand it, they would want the notoriety. Sure, they wear sheets and do damage at night, but want their actions to be known. First there were threatening letters in her mailbox. Then about what time in the morning did they burn the cross?"

"She said it was around one a.m.," Hawk said. "They did some damage to the Shorts' other properties the next night. Guess because they rented the house to her. After the letter, the Sheriff's department requested the night deputies do extra patrol in the area."

A slight disgust was in his voice when Father replied, "That doesn't do much good. All they would have to do is sit back off the road to watch the patrol pass. Only have to wait a short time before doing their damage. An idiot could figure that out."

They heard a car pull into the drive. Both went to the window to see who it was.

Ron, Wilber, and both Shorts got out to come in. Father opened the door to welcome them.

Ron remarked, "Kinda thought you might be here talking with Father. We're going to get a bunch of guys and catch them in the act tonight. Thought you might join us."

Father reached into the closet to get a folding chair. Offering one to Wilber he said, "You boys know where the refrigerator is. Help yourselves. I'm having my mint tea. Sis brought fresh mint this morning."

When everyone sat down, Father asked, "So what's your plan?"

Wilber was first to speak. "We kinda think they'll be back tonight. We're gonna be ready for them."

"Yeah!" Ron chipped in. "Hawk, we wanta use your drive for one staging area to wait in our trucks. Then there's plenty of room down there as you turn off to enter Quaintberg Estates for two or three more trucks to wait. We could hem them in.

We have to set up some sort of communication system so we all move at the same time, closing in on them from both directions. Also, need lookouts to advise us when they're in the area."

Father was curious and asked, "And when you catch them, how are you going to handle it? Best you hold them some way and call the sheriff's office."

"Way they messed up my place, I'd like to mess them up a little bit," John Short said, "Take them over to my house and let them scrub off the paint they put on my garage door. If the paint doesn't come off the door, we could scrub them with Brillo pads."

"Take them over to Miss Fanny Ruff's, and make them apologize on bended knee over and over," Ron suggested. "Maybe hold 'em and let her slap them around awhile. You're coming with, right, Father?"

Father's smile was questionable as he said, "Think I'd better sit this one out. I'd like to see this stopped, but that's not why I was assigned here. You guys do be careful how you handle them because of the law. Quaintberg has been too much in the news already."

Hawk stood. "Father's right. I don't think they would ever do anything to St. Francis church or the rectory. Why don't we all go down to the Quaintberg Tavern and discuss this farther? I like your guys' idea to catch them."

They all stood and followed Hawk out the door as they said goodnight to Father.

Word was out, and several men met at the Quaintberg Tavern. It was agreed that three trucks would be staged at the entrance to Wright Farm. Another three would be at Quaintberg Estates. At Wright Farm the guard would receive phone calls and report to them. At Quaintberg Estates, Derick was to get the phone calls. Each truck was to be driven by one man and one man with a rifle was to be in the bed of each truck. They finished their drinks and departed for their assigned positions to wait.

Meantime Father noticed that two cars had pulled up and stopped at the west side of the general store. Soon another car with two young men arrived, and another with three men. Two motorcycles pulled up and stopped. The men left their cars and grouped behind the store so Father couldn't see them. Father knew Rob and Emmie Lou had gone to Poplar Bluff and felt he must alert the men, so he called the guard at Wright Farm. Quickly Ron returned the call. Ron's instructions to Father were to stay inside. He would contact the other men, and they would all block Quaintberg Road. He told Father that one man would be driving each truck and one man would be standing in the bed of the truck with a gun pointed toward the group. Finally he said, "Now Father, you talk better than any of us. When you see we've blocked the road, you go over and talk with them. If they give you any trouble just get out of the way. We'll take over."

Father's heart was beating fast as he waited. In a short amount of time six pickup trucks arrived totally blocking any way for the young men to escape. Father was out of the house, and ran across the road calling out, "Hey! What are you guys doing? You're in big trouble."

The young men rushed from the rear of the building to see the pickup trucks with guns pointed in their direction. Their eyes almost popped out of the sockets. Their hearts raced. Some broke out in cold sweat. Others trembled.

One young man stammered, "Oh! Please! We aren't doing anything wrong. We're just waiting here for a couple more guys. We'll leave now. Honest."

Father saw the fear and believed the young man. He asked, "What are your plans?"

There was sweat on the young man's forehead as he explained, "Our buddy's parents moved to Quaintberg Estates about three weeks ago. He's getting married. We chose to meet here to go as a group. We wanted to give him a surprise stag party."

By this time the pickup trucks had moved forward to circle the building. A few jumped out in time to hear the young man. The crowd had banded together for protection. The men from Quaintberg began to laugh, but not the young men. They stood silent.

The spokesman said, "Sir, please. If you let us go we'll leave right now. We're sorry. Didn't think meeting here would hurt anything. Honest."

Wilber stepped forward to say, "Boys, we didn't know why you were congregating here. Now you can stay, but better leave when your other buddies arrive."

John Short's driver backed his truck to leave an opening for the cars. Seeing this, the young men rushed to their cars to start the motors.

Ron called, "Fellows. Wait! Wait here for the rest of the guys."

The lead car headed for the opening to escape, and the others followed.

The Quaintberg men stood around awhile talking, joking and laughing at the mistake before returning to their assigned positions.

Father put on a stack of seventy-eight records for him and Deek to listen to as he tried to relax. Sinatra was his favorite. Especially *New York, New York* and *Chicago.*

He dozed off to be awakened by a knock at his back door. Deek jumped off the couch barking and rushed to it. Father flipped on the porch light as he opened the door.

A woman's voice cried, "Please turn off the light. I need help. Please let me in."

The moonlight was obscured by low lying clouds, but Father did as the woman suggested. He pushed the door open wider and invited, "Come on in. Who are you?

When she was in his dimly-lit kitchen he was shocked to see her face. It was cut, swollen and bruised. She was lightly crying but said, "Norma Wilddo. I don't know no place else to go for help. I live in the ol' yellow trailer back down the hill in the woods."

First he handed her his handkerchief, and then took her by the arm to lead her into the living area. "Who did that to your face?"

Still sobbing, she said, "Buster, my husband. He got out of the pen about two months ago, and found I had left St. Louis. I moved down here in my boyfriend's ol' trailer. Buster showed up here two weeks ago. He beat me and my boyfriend. Then he took him for a ride. Don't know where he is. I look so bad I can't even go to my job at the dime store in Javelle. I don't know what I'm gonna do. He and his friends, Frank and Gene, did all the damage to that black woman's home and everywhere. They're just mean. They're down there playin' cards and drinkin'. They gots a plan. Sometime tonight Frank's to drive by her house and shoot it. Then he'll keep going. They're expecting the police to come investigate. While they're busy there, Buster and Gene will break into the Gruder Wine

Store. I'm scared. When they find out I'm not in bed, they'll come lookin' for me."

Father had sat quietly listening. Then he got up to say, "You're trembling. Let me get you a throw to put around you. You're okay. You'll be safe here with me."

"I don't know what to do. Where to go."

"Right now," he said, handing her the throw, "you're going to stay right here. They don't know where you are, and doubt they would come here to look. I must call the sheriff's office. Would you like water, tea or I could make coffee?"

She shook her head no.

Walking toward the kitchen, he said, "Relax."

He was surprised when Deputy Duck answered the phone. Deputy Duck listened as Father related the story. Then he asked, "Father, is she where she might hear my voice?"

"No," Father replied.

Deputy Duck continued, "Good. The reason I'm back here tonight is that a man was out coon hunting. He found a young man's body in the woods off Highway M. It just may be the man she called her boyfriend." There was a pause before Deputy Duck said, "Father, I'll be right out there with another deputy or two. We'll be driving unmarked cars. Keep her with you and your lights low. Don't tell anyone she's with you. No one. There's enough on them to arrest now, but I'd rather catch them in the act. The other deputies will stay just west of the black woman's house. He has to fire the gun before we can bring him in, but they will. Call the owners of the wine store. Tell them only enough to get them to wait for us in the store with the lights off and the door unlocked. No guns. I'd better get going now."

When Father returned to the living area the young woman had lain down and was asleep on the couch. Her arm was over Deek who made himself comfortable next to her.

The music stopped. Father waited in silence until he heard a car in his drive. He opened the door to allow Deputy Duck to enter, and it woke the young woman. Father introduced them, but Deputy Duck appeared to be in a hurry.

"Keep the lights low or off," he said. "Ma'am, you stay inside and keep the doors locked. Don't answer the door or phone. Father, you want to come with me? I'd like that, if you don't mind. I don't know the other men. There's two deputies waiting for the guy who is to fire at the black woman's house."

Father said, "I'll go with you. Let me get my boots." Then he turned to Norma, "Remember what the deputy said. Don't answer the door or the phone. If Deek barks, let him bark. That would indicate he's here alone."

After hiding Deputy Duck's car in back of the wine store, they entered the front door. Mr. Gruder and Frank Talaman, his partner, rose from behind the counter. After the introductions were made, and the front door locked, there was nothing to do but wait.

The wait was only about twenty five minutes. First they heard the shot. It was followed by lights flashing and sirens sounding. In no time pickup trucks were rushing past the wine store not knowing the deputy was there.

"Guess it won't be long now," Deputy Duck said in a low voice. I suggest you two men just stay behind the counter. Get down if any bullets are fired. Father, you get on the one side of the door and I'll be on the other. Let them walk in before I announce they're under arrest. If they try and run, I think you can handle one. Right? Gruder, you stand by the light switch. When I say on, flip it."

Everyone took their positions as Father said, "After seeing that young woman's face, I'd just like to know which one did it."

The wait was short. They heard the car stop in front. It sounded like two men exited and left the motor running. Fast steps were heard. Someone crashed the glass in the door. An arm reached around and turned the lock allowing them to enter. Both were rushing toward the cash-register on the counter when Deputy Duck commanded, "On!"

Lights on, Deputy Duck announced, "Hold it. You're under arrest." One man stopped with his hands up, but the other headed toward Father and the door.

"Buster?" Father called loudly.

The response from the running man was an automatic "yes?"

Father drew back his arm and swung forward with a closed fist to hit Buster smack in the face. Buster fell backward, landing straddle-legged on his back on the floor.

Deputy Duck was handcuffing the other man, but, laughing, said, "Father, I asked if you could handle that one."

Father rubbed the skinned knuckles on his right hand, and said, "Oh. I misunderstood. I thought you said I should hand him one."

Chapter 20

The Men's Club completed the new pavilion and cook-shack between the church and hall. The cook-shack was designed so the men could fry chicken or fish, grill and barbeque. It was all completed in time to use for the upcoming 3rd annual picnic.

Father used the pavilion to sit outside to read, write, or visit. To do so in good weather was to be expected; however, he also enjoyed chilly weather and warm rainy days. When Hawk and Marg became aware of his liking for it, they added a small storage area at one end to hold folding-chairs. Many a meal he would prepare for himself to carry to the pavilion to eat. Deek, too, found it to be a great place. At the pavilion, Father felt free to now and then drop a bite of his food for Deek.

Often Father sat there with his iced tea, and pondered about how many gallons of his mint-lemon tea he served in the past three years. It was a favorite drink of many when they visited. Some of the men, like Ron, who once only drank beer was switching. He gave away boxes and jars of his tea blends to all his friends. There was one blend for cold and another for hot. Sis was his only supplier of both fresh and dried mint. He chuckled, recalling how his secret receipt for chili was popular at all the church events. People suggest he package his tea and chili seasoning mixes to sell at the next annual picnic. He knew it would be possible to package the teas; however, no one knew of the alcoholic beverage he added to his chili mixture, especially the members of The Assembly of God Church, who raved about it. Their pastor, after finishing the second helping, once remarked that if it couldn't be boxed, he should have it canned to sell.

He and Pastor Allgood of The Assembly of God church become friends when together they started a food pantry for the needy in the area. They used a portion of the basement of The Assembly Of God Church to distribute food every Tuesday. On that day, Father and Pastor Allgood usually just walked around greeting those who came.

Volunteers from both churches worked together to prepare bags of groceries to give to the needy. Each time when the pantry closed Father, Pastor Allgood, and his wife would serve sandwiches and salads or soups to the volunteers back in St. Francis Hall. More of Father's tea was drunk than the milk or soda. When he had extra tea bagged he would give packages to the ladies from The Assembly of God who asked for them, but he never gave away his recipes for his teas or chili.

A car with the county symbol on the side turned off PP onto Quaintberg Road. He watched as it stopped in his drive. A young woman wearing a navy blue business suit got out.

He called to her from the pavilion, "I'm down here. Come join me."

As she held her badge for him to see, she said, "I'm Sue Seetoem, a county social-worker. I'm looking for Hellga Crazes. I was told she lives by the cemetery. Do you know her?"

Father stood to pour her a glass of tea. "Have a seat, and try my tea. I don't know her. In fact, to the best of my knowledge, I've never seen her, but think I know where she lives."

The tea was inviting, and Sue sat down. "I was told she's living alone. Her son, Clem, dropped off a note requesting we check on her. Said he was leaving town for good." She hesitated before saying, "I'm a little concerned about going there alone. His note said she's crazy, mean, and could be dangerous. That was his reasons for leaving."

Father smiled and said, "Although I don't know her, I've heard a few stories. I doubt they're true. Some say she talks with the dead. Several believe she's a true witch. Mr. Gruder told me she once put a hex on his cows, and they never produced a calf that spring. Of course, it's not true."

She appeared nervous when she asked, "Where is the road? I didn't see any by a cemetery."

"It's not a road as such," he said, standing. "It's more like a farmer's lane through the field that leads back into the woods. I've nothing special to do now. If you like, I'll drive you back there. I'd like to see her myself. I just need to put Deek in the house."

"Father, I'd sure appreciate it," Sue said. "By the way, your tea is delicious."

After Father drove across the field and entered the woods, they learned a vehicle couldn't go any farther. A long walking-path through the woods, overgrown with vines, led to a rundown, never-painted small shack. In the distance two old dogs behind a fence announced their arrival. The smell of unhealthy, penned animals and manure became more rancid with each step.

They heard a door slam before a weak, hoarse voice called, "Hold up thar! You'd be on my property. Better have reason. If'en you's don't, I's ready to pump lead in your belly."

As they reached the gate, they could see Hellga Crazes standing on the porch with a shotgun pointed in their direction. On her head was a filthy man's hat, soiled from years of sweat and dirt. Salt and pepper gray, dirty, matted hair dangled beneath it, down her back and around her face. She wore a faded flowered dress with a multitude of stains that had seen many a year of wear and infrequent washings. It was immense on her small frame and hung uneven to her ankles. Even though it was warm she wore a ratty gray sweater with one pocket almost torn off. It was impossible to tell the color of her work shoes since they were worn and covered with a mixture of straw, manure, and mud.

Closer yet, they could see the stains on her lips from her chewing tobacco. The juices had leaked from her mouth and dried around her protruding, long, hairy chin.

Father called, "Father Bill from the Catholic Church. Do you mind if Sue and I come to visit?"

She hesitated a time before she leaned the gun against the wall. She called back, "A priest, you say? God man. Reckon to be right, since finished skinnin' my rabbit. Gots all the stuff ready cookin' for the stew. Dang rabbits gettin' harder and harder to catch. Figure that stew gonna last a few days. That'll be 'bout the time Clem gets back here with somethin' else. Him's always run off. Clay, not at all like his brother. Always 'round."

Sue looked at Father. "So she does have one son with her?"

He kept his voice low to answer. "Guess so. I know nothing about them."

As they moved in from the gate, Hellga stepped off the porch and sat on it. Her eyes were almost closed with heavy eyelids. Although the sun was in her face, causing her to squint, she kept focused on them as they came toward her.

The invitation was not friendly when she stated, "You's can sit a spell here on the porch, if you'n like. Clay don't like no company in the house."

They chose to stand in front of her. Father positioned himself to shade her face with his body when he asked, "Clay? Is he your husband?"

She slapped her hand on her leg as if it were a joke. "Gracious no! Him's my baby boy. Me thinks he got choked on one of dem fish bones. Don't know where they takes his body. Make no difference. He come back home to me."

Sue and Father looked at each other in wonder. Carefully, Sue asked, "Where is he now?"

Hellga looked back toward a window, and said, "If he not peering at you's, he maybe sleepin'. We's had a bad night. Times I can't find him."

Having slipped a little note pad and pencil from her purse, Sue said, "Mrs. Crazes, it's not good for you living here alone. It'll take a few days to make the arrangements, but the county will take care of you. The homes are very nice. I have a few questions; however I'm certain you qualify."

Hellga struggled to stand. Without a word she walked away from them and around the side of the house. She returned with a dirty, grey, rotting board, about two feet long in her hands, prepared to swing. "Now youse git! Git out'ta here. Ain't gitting' my place." She was right in front of Sue shaking the board. "I said, GIT!"

Sue backed up, turned and rushed to the gate. Father stood watching, believing she was not angry with him. He called, "Sue, go wait in the car. I'll be there in a few minutes."

Hellga rested the board on the ground with one hand. The other was on her hip as she squared off at Father. "I'll be puttin' a hex on that one. She no come back here ever. What you want? Go!"

Instead of leaving, Father sat on the porch, and patted a place for Helga. "Here. Sit with me. You have a nice place, but I would bet it's a lot of work for you. You're getting along in years. With Clem gone, and I'd bet Clay doesn't help much—you're carrying a heavy load."

Hellga didn't sit, but he read her body language to be relaxed. She stared at him and he back at her. To the side she spit tobacco juice onto the ground before turning her head sideways. "Clay and me thinks you be smart. We thinks we could trust you."

Father smiled. "Clay has good judgment." He stood to say, "That sun is getting hot. Why don't you go back into the house now? I'll take that woman away from here. He extended his hand, "You know, I like you. Would you mind if I came back to visit again?"

He was hoping for a smile, but instead Hellga wiped her hands on her skirt a couple time before checking them. "Too dirty for you to shake. You bein' nice and all."

Father grabbed her hand and held it for a short time as he said, "That's not true. I have a special respect for hands that worked hard. I'll be seeing you soon."

Back in his car, he suggested Sue go ahead with plans to move Hellga into a state facility, but wait for his call to move her. He planned to work with Hellga to change her mind.

Before he made the second visit he went into Javelle to purchase food, soaps and paper products for her with his own money since the pantry wouldn't have all the items she needed. Then he stopped at the pharmacy for face masks to wear when he made his visits. He could explain them to Hellga by saying he had allergies

Walking down the path to the gate he saw Hellga, dressed in the same garb she was wearing on his last visit. Her back was to him as she worked with a long, thin, brown dead dog lying on the porch. He called, "Mrs. Crazes. Father Bill. I come to visit." As he closed the gate he laughingly said, "The mask. I'm not coming to hold you up. I have allergies."

She turned her head only to say, "Well, com'on. Buck be ready soon. Help carry him to the hole." She was dipping a large tooth comb into a wash-pan of water and combing his hair. Now and then she would cast off a flea or tick. Found him last night. I done dug a hole behind ol' barn. Him's about ready to go up yonder."

Father wished to be kind, and said, "He'll be waiting for you there."

Hilga stopped, rubbed her hand on her skirt, looked straight at Father to pronounce, "Not me. I'm devil child. Marked when born." She reached to pull her upper lip toward her nose to expose a mouth of rotten and missing teeth. "See."

It was enough to turn his stomach, but he asked, "See what?"

With the other hand she pointed to her two buck teeth, "The sign. Dem first teeth never touched. Big wide spread. True Devil child. Am."

He was stunned and wished for time, so he suggested, "Let's take Buck and bury him. Then we can talk."

After placing the groceries on the porch, he sat two chairs in the shade for them which he had purchased along with the groceries.

"Mrs. Crazes, I don't know who told you about you being a child of the Devil, but they were wrong. Dead wrong. God loves you. God loves all people. You're not a child of the Devil. You're God's child. I swear to that."

She sat silent for awhile before she turned to look into his face. Her head then turned to look back down at her lap before bending forward to place her out-stretched hands between her legs as if in thought. She leaned farther forward.

Shaking her head, her voice was low when she said, "Nobody want me. Ol' grandma hate takin' care of me, but no choice. No like my babies. Trade me to Mr. Kinkerfuss, so she gets place when he die. She die first. It's mine."

Only wishing to say something, he asked, "Was he good to you?"

He could hear her weeping and watched her body as it trembled. She muttered, "He no allow 'em kinfolk mens to use me anymore. He old. No bother at all."

Father placed his chair close to put his hand on her shoulder. "You're all right now. Safe. I've sat three bags of groceries on the porch for you." He stood. "You must be tired. I'll go now, but will be back soon. God will always be with you. Remember that. You're God's child: not the Devil's. That's true. Believe it. Get rid of that Devil thought. The days ahead will be real good. I promise."

She responded, "I want's to believe you. I do."

As he walked toward his car he kept looking back but she didn't move.

He made two more visits, and after each, reported to Sue on his progress. Sue told him a facility was ready for her.

As he drove over for the fifth trip he prayed that it would be his last. Never did he mention to her that the move would be permanent, but in his opinion, she was ready for a little get-away rest.

He parked the car and walked down the path. She was not in view and didn't answer his call. He was careful as he walked around the house and out to the sheds. She was nowhere in sight. He took in a deep breath and exhaled. There was no choice but to enter the house. After he placed a second mask over the first, he opened the door to step inside. Hellga was lying fully clothed on an old soiled mattress on the floor. Piles of rags and feed sacks strewn about may have been used to keep her warm. Her eyes were closed, but she was wheezing. He believed there was nothing he personally could do, so he backed out and closed the door.

Back at the rectory he placed a call for an ambulance to come take her to the emergency room at St. Joseph Hospital in Poplar Bluff. Next was a call to Sue to alert her of what was happening. He promised to sit in his car on Highway PP to wait for the ambulance, so they would not miss the turn to Hellga's house. When he was certain she was in the ambulance, he went directly to the church. He knelt before the altar and asked God to make her well so she would get to know and love Him as he did.

Three days later he met Sue and together they went to St. Joseph Hospital. They barely recognized Hellga. She was lying on her back on snowy white sheets. A sky blue blanket was pulled just above her waist. The clean, cut, salt and pepper hair had a sheen to it. The parts of her light blue eyes showing shined with a new life. Her face had been scrubbed clean to expose smooth skin. Sue suspected the clean, blue-green hospital gown was the first clean thing to touch her skin in many a year. Her smile was welcomed sunshine.

She slipped one hand from under the cover to extend to Father Bill as she said, "Father Bill, you's right. I do feel likes I done died and gone to Heaven."

Chapter 21

After saying his prayers, Father lay in bed recalling his blessings. George Enstruckee, the treasurer for the third annual picnic, left only an hour before, after reporting the profit was forty percent better than last year. The beautiful weather played a big part in an increased attendance. He knew the workers were tired, yet they were always willing to work. He hadn't heard one complaint. Again, he thanked God for all his blessings and fell asleep.

He was awakened with a severe headache. He thought he must have in some way turned in his sleep and twisted his back because of the back pain. The day before, after a visit to the hospital, he experienced flu-like symptoms, but chose to ignore them. Stumbling around he found the clock on the nightstand. It was only five twenty-five. There was nothing in his medicine cabinet to ease the headache. The pain in his back was becoming more severe which caused him to fill the tub with hot water, thinking it would take the pain away.

Instead of getting into the tub, he put on his clothes, knowing he was in trouble. He hoped the Bleu's might be up and dialed their number. After four rings Rob answered, "Yes! Who's calling?"

Father wincing with pain and stammered, "Rob, Father Bill. I hate to bother you, but no one else to call. Man, I'm hurting. I'm sick. Could you...?"

Father was doubled up and lying on the floor when both Rob and Emmie Lou, still in her night clothes, arrived to help him. Rob reached down with intentions to help him on the couch, but Father screamed with pain. "Please, no. No. I can't move. My back—and I have a terrible headache."

Rob ordered, "Emmie Lou, call for an ambulance! Tell 'em to get out here—damn quick!"

While they waited for the ambulance Rob paced the floor praying Father would be all right. After awhile the groaning slowed. They observed his body jerk violently while his eyes at times opened and rolled back into his head before they closed.

Emmie Lou knelt beside him with a cool washcloth placed on his head. She remarked, "His temperature must be real high. I feel so helpless."

"Where's that damn ambulance?" Rob asked. "I'm waiting outside."

With Rob on one side and Emmie Lou on the other, they talked to Father as the men carried him on the stretcher to the ambulance. One of the men requested, "Please let us get him in the ambulance. He doesn't hear you. He's unconscious."

In tears Emmie Lou said, "But he's all right. He keeps moving his arms. God, where are you! Please help us."

While Emmie Lou completed dressing so she and Rob could go to the hospital, Rob called the Goodmans. He told them about Father Bill, and requested when they had time to check things in the rectory. Possibly they could find a key to lock the door and take care of the dog.

As the men with the ambulance pushed Father Bill into the emergency room he was convulsing, intermittently groaning and flinging his arms about. Shots of Phenobarbitol slowed his squirming and bursts of garbled sounds.

The tests began. When a lumbar puncture was performed for a small amount of cerebrospinal fluid, they realized from the color it was indicating an infection—Meningitis. More tests were performed in an attempt to learn if it was viral or bacterial Meningitis. They were pleased that at times he was fighting with both sides equally under the straps on the stretcher to keep him down. After a battery of x-ray, a breathing tube was put into his trachea, taking the job of breathing away from him. In the intensive nursing care area on the third floor a battery of monitors sat around his bed.

Two other doctors were consulted before a call was placed to a specialist at Barnes Hospital in St. Louis. About two hours passed before he became quiet.

The Goodmans had alerted several parishioners and they called others. Many from Quaintberg crowded the waiting room and hall. The attending doctor came from his room, and asked, "Who is here that I may talk with about Father Bill McHeck's condition?"

Derick Dejesus spoke up, "Sir, he has no relatives in this area. We're his friends and parishioners."

The doctor raised his hands and motioned for them to come closer to announce, "From the test performed we have learned he may have bacterial meningitis. I just spoke with a specialist at Barnes Hospital in St. Louis. They have newer and better equipment for this, plus a battery of specialists. He's being prepared for the trip as every minute counts. Is there anyone who can contact his family?"

Big Jane spoke out, "Yes, I've already called his mother. I'll let her know he's being moved."

They gathered on the parking lot to talk. A few chose to return home, but a number chose to make the two plus hour ride to St. Louis. Arriving in St. Louis, in the waiting room they met Father Bill's mother and grandmother. Rebecca McHeck talked with Bishop Gunn. After a long wait a doctor came to speak with them. He said, "We're doing all we can. He's in a coma. It's all right now if anyone wishes to go into his room. Our policy is no more than two people at a time. Visiting hours are from ten a.m. until eight p.m."

John Short, from the back called, "I'd like to stay here through the night."

Shaking his head the doctor replied, "I'm sorry. That's against policy."

Rebecca Heck standing in the middle of the group stepped forward. When she was right in front of the doctor she announced, "That's my grandson in there. I want him to know we're here. There will always be someone with him through every night. That's my policy! Tell that to your administrator."

With flushed face the doctor turned to leave. Bishop Gunn caught up with him. The crowd watched as the two walked away conferring quietly.

Bill's mother and grandmother were first to enter. His mother found a chair for Rebecca so she could sit close and hold Bill's hand. His mother stood on the opposite side on his bed until later when a nurse brought in another chair.

Meanwhile, Marg sent Hawk to find a gift-shop to purchase pencils and small note books so a schedule for those volunteering to sit with him could be made.

Almost a half hour passed before Bishop Gunn returned to announce he had met with the administrator. Permission was granted that anyone who wished could stay the night.

Hawk took the floor to announce, "When Father Bill's family comes out a schedule can be made for those who choose to sit with him. The two Mrs. McHecks will have first choice. Then there'll be a need for volunteers for the extra time."

Rebecca, having heard Bishop Gunn's voice came out to listen. She didn't hesitate to add, "Talk if you like...pray...sit silent, but always hold his hand. Let him know we'll never let him go. Never, I say."

There was no shortage of volunteers. Some drove back and forth from Quaintberg while others stayed in St. Louis. Hawk rented a suite at the Chase Hotel for him and Marg with two bedrooms, two baths, and a sitting room with a couch which made into a bed. He made it clear that it was available to anyone wishing to use it.

Day two came and went as did days three and four with no good news. In fact, it was starting to sink in that all their hopes and prayers were not going to be answered. Sometimes a person sitting with him might think they saw some sign of movement and would call a nurse, only to be told a person in a coma often acts that way because of muscle activity.

Morning of the fifth day no one was aware that Father Bill's spirit had separated from his mind and body. It floated upward as if the ceiling and floors didn't exist. From that position he was able to watch and listen to the people below— parishioners from St. Francis of Assisi, friends from his school years, neighbors, Archbishop Cannon, his mother and his grandmother, Rebecca McHeck. A few were gathered in small circles talking. John Short had fallen asleep in a chair. Others hugged and wiped tears. Some teens sat on the floor in the hall, reading or playing games. Kate and Marg were taking their turns to sit on opposite sides of the bed and hold his hands. It was a good representation of his family and friends he loved so much.

A doctor approached and requested his mother and grandmother come with him as he needed to talk with them. Respectfully, the crowd stayed away as they huddled around the corner.

Father Bill was able to listen as the doctor began, "I'm sorry to have to tell you this but we have done all we can do. Truthfully we are surprised he hasn't passed before now. Most with this disease die within 24 to 48 hours. This is the fifth day. Each day we have seen more loss. Now, it would be a miracle should he survive. We do know that the bacterium begins early to destroy the brain. I'm sorry."

His mother was wiping away a few tears. His grandmother stood firm staring straight. After a short period of silence, he said, "Follow me. Let's go into the room. I'll ask the other ladies to leave his bedside, so you can be alone with him."

Tears were falling down his mother's cheeks while his grandmother appeared to be in shock when they walked toward the crowd and into his room. As the doctor exited the room, he motioned for the other ladies to come with him. Before Kate turned loose of Bill's hand his grandmother grabbed it. On the other side his mother held his hand in both of hers.

Bill wished for a way to communicate with them, but knew he was removed from any activity on earth.

He watched when Rebecca McHeck stood, stretched erect, and took a deep breath. She squeezed his hand with all her might. It almost stopped the circulation in his fingers. She began shaking it so hard it vibrated his arm all the way to his shoulder.

With the firmest voice she could muster she demanded, "Sonny boy, this is your grandmother! Don't you dare to go to Heaven before me! I insist I go first. And don't you dare act like you don't hear me! You know I have big ears and an eye in the back of my head. Now you'd better listen to me." Her legs gave away and she melted to the floor, but never let go of his hand.

Bill was laughing so hard at her spunk, he believed if his spirit had been connected to his mind and body the bed would be wet.

All contact with the earth disappeared. It was as if someone flipped a switch. He was in total darkness—best described as pitch black. A black deeper than any he'd ever experienced or was ever told about; however, he was not afraid. In the far distance, a pin-head light with a strong beam was pointing toward him. He was wondering if he was floating to the light or it was coming to him. Instantly he was in the light. There were sounds of beautiful music, more beautiful than any orchestra he'd ever heard. Never had he ever felt on earth that he was not loved, but this love around him was greater than any he believed could be. All love! Beautiful colors floated about him. They could not be matched by the finest artists. He remembered nothing about his life on earth as he basked in this new world. Words in the English language were not sufficient to describe it. Something or someone took his hand.

An angelic male voice declared, "Bill, I wanted you to see this, but it's not your time to stay."

About the author

Wynn Melton has had short stories and essays published in various small presses. He won 2nd place in *Oasis* magazine's short story contest in 2014 for best fiction. He lives in St. Clair, Missouri.

CPSIA information can be obtained
at www.ICGtesting.com
Printed in the USA
FSHW02n0802100618
49253FS